"I Don't Care How You Entertain The Kid. Just Do It. And Leave Me Out Of It."

Anna's face blanched, making her freckles stand out. Pierce experienced a sudden craving for cinnamon toast—the way his mother used to make it twenty-something years ago.

He shook his head to banish the thought.

"Yessir." She turned away to attend to the kid.

Feeling as if he'd kicked a kitten, Pierce grabbed his plate and a bottle of water and retreated to his office. He'd hired her to deal with the trivial childcare issues. He didn't need her or her sleepy, sexy—no, not sexy—morning eyes condemning him.

What she didn't seem to realize was that the kid would be better off if Pierce kept his distance.

Dear Reader,

When my editor asked if I'd like to write a Billionaires and Babies story, I didn't hesitate to say yes. Who doesn't love babies?

Except my hero, of course!

My sons are all long past the cuddly stage, and I've reached a point where I actually miss their squabbling and wrestling. For those of you who are still dealing with kiddie chaos, rest assured, your day to miss the madness will come all too soon.

I loved having the opportunity to throw not one, but two tiny tots at my baby-phobic hero and watching them (and Anna, the boys' nanny) win him over. I hope you enjoy watching Pierce succumb to Anna and the pint-size charmers, too.

I enjoy hearing from readers! Please contact me through my website, www.emilierose.com.

Happy reading!

Emilie Rose

EMILIE ROSE

THE TIES THAT BIND

™ **Harlequin**®

Desire

Recycling programs
for this product may
not exist in your area.

ISBN-13: 978-0-373-73170-1

THE TIES THAT BIND

www.Harlequin.com

Printed in U.S.A.

Books by Emilie Rose

Harlequin Desire

Her Tycoon to Tame #2112
The Price of Honor #2124
The Ties that Bind #2157

Silhouette Desire

Forbidden Passion #1624
Breathless Passion #1635
Scandalous Passion #1660
Condition of Marriage #1675
*Paying the Playboy's Price #1732
*Exposing the Executive's Secrets #1738
*Bending to the Bachelor's Will #1744
Forbidden Merger #1753
†The Millionaire's Indecent Proposal #1804
†The Prince's Ultimate Deception #1810
†The Playboy's Passionate Pursuit #1817
Secrets of the Tycoon's Bride #1831
**Shattered by the CEO #1871
**Bound by the Kincaid Baby #1881
**Wed by Deception #1894
Pregnant on the Upper East Side? #1903
Bargained Into Her Boss's Bed #1934
‡More Than a Millionaire #1963
‡Bedding the Secret Heiress #1973
‡His High-Stakes Holiday Seduction #1980
Executive's Pregnancy Ultimatum #1994
Wedding His Takeover Target #2048

*Trust Fund Affairs
†Monte Carlo Affairs
**The Payback Affairs
‡The Hightower Affairs

Other titles by this author
available in ebook format

EMILIE ROSE

Bestselling Harlequin Desire author and RITA® Award finalist Emilie Rose lives in her native North Carolina with her four sons and two adopted mutts. Writing is her third (and hopefully her last) career. She's managed a medical office and run a home day care, neither of which offers half as much satisfaction as plotting happy endings. Her hobbies include gardening and cooking (especially cheesecake). She's a rabid country music fan because she can find an entire book in almost any song. She is currently working her way through her own "bucket list," which includes learning to ride a Harley. Visit her website at www.emilierose.com or email EmilieRoseC@aol.com. Letters can be mailed to P.O. Box 20145, Raleigh, NC 27619.

To the men and women of our military
who sacrifice so much so that the rest of us
can stay home with our families.

One

Anna Aronson aimed a measured breath at the plastic wand and wished the bubbles exiting the opposite side could magically carry her worries away on the breeze.

The boys playing at her feet in the thick emerald grass squealed and gurgled in the infectious way only toddlers can, making her smile despite impending disaster.

She had to get this job.

A flash of movement caught her attention. She glanced away from the boys scampering after the bubbles, and spotted the woman who'd interviewed her earlier coming toward them. Tension wound inside Anna like an Archimedean spiral.

"Mr. Hollister will see you now, Anna. He's waiting in his office. Take the doors on the left side of the patio." She gestured to the luxurious, sprawling Greenwich, Connecticut, home.

Anna licked her dry lips and lowered the wand. "The boys…"

"I'll watch them while you talk to the boss. He has the final say. But for what it's worth, you have my vote." Mrs. Findley held out her hand for the bottle of bubbles and wand.

Anna, feeling as if she were surrendering a life preserver in rough seas, handed them over. This interview felt very much like a sink or swim situation. If she didn't get this job she wouldn't be able to pay this month's rent or electric bill, and she'd be left with no option except to swallow her pride, go home and beg for help even though her mother had already made it clear that Anna and Cody would not be welcome in the retirement community where she resided.

But hopefully it wouldn't come to that. "Thank you, Mrs. Findley."

"Call me Sarah. And, Anna, don't let Pierce intimidate you. He's a fair employer and a good man despite the armor plated personality."

Armor plated personality?

Trepidation closed Anna's throat. She couldn't have spoken even if an appropriate response had materialized in her seized up brain. Instead she nodded and headed for the house. The distance seemed endless, and by the time she reached the stone porch stairs of the two-story colonial her breaths came quickly—as if she'd run a mile instead of walking a few hundred yards.

Through the glass door Anna spotted her prospective employer sitting behind a massive wooden desk. The air jammed in her lungs. Please, please, please let this go well.

She knocked on the glass. He looked up from a stack of papers, scowling, then bid her to enter with one sharp snap of his head. Her hand slipped on the polished brass knob. She had to blot her damp palm on her dress before trying again and pushing open the door.

Pierce Hollister, with his supermodel chiseled features and thick, dark hair styled in one of those intentionally messy cuts, looked as if he belonged in a glossy magazine advertisement for an expensive product that any young millionaire might want to buy, and though he'd dressed casually in a black polo shirt opened at the base of his tanned neck, he still reeked of power and prestige.

But a handsome, charming, wealthy man had contributed to her current financial predicament. She couldn't afford to let her guard down with this one.

"H-hello, Mr. Hollister. I'm Anna Aronson."

Hazel eyes without a trace of friendliness inspected her from head to toe. She hoped her simple shirt dress and sandals passed muster.

"Why were you fired from your last position?"

Flustered by the terse question even before she'd closed the door, she bought time by focusing on the—ohmigod original—art on the walls around him and pushing the door until she heard the lock catch. So much for a polite handshake greeting.

"I was let go because I refused an after school playdate with the father of one of my students."

"He propositioned you?"

"Yes."

"Why didn't you file a complaint with the headmaster?"

"I did. But the parent in question is one of the school's primary benefactors and his wife is their most successful fundraiser. My complaint was ignored."

"How long did you work for the school?"

"The dates are in my resume."

"I'm asking you."

Why would he question her credentials unless he thought she'd made them up and wouldn't recall them? "The academy hired me part-time straight out of college as a tutor for some of their struggling students. Six months later when a teacher quit unexpectedly they offered me a full-time teaching position. All totaled I worked for the school for three and a half years."

"And despite your history as an employee the school fired you because of one parent's allegations. They chose to take his word over yours."

"The headmaster believed generous private school donors were harder to come by than elementary school teachers."

"Or perhaps they were looking for an excuse to get rid of you because you weren't good enough."

The unjust allegation stole her breath. "I've received exemplary evaluations at every review and the salary increases to go with it."

"And if I call the school to verify your story?"

Her hopes sank. He didn't believe her. He wasn't the first. And until someone did she'd never find a job that would pay enough to cover decent day care for Cody while she worked. Maybe if she could pick up more students to tutor and college papers to edit she could make ends meet…

Who are you trying to fool? That won't be enough.

She fought the urge to fidget beneath his condemning stare. "If you call the school you will be told the parent in question said I picked on his son unmercifully after he—the father—refused my advances."

"Did you make advances?"

She jerked in surprise. No one had asked that before. "Of course not. He's married."

"Married men have affairs."

"Not with me they don't."

"Your resume states you graduated with honors from Vanderbilt. My assistant tells me that's one of the best education programs in the country. How is it you can't find a teaching position?"

This felt more like an interrogation than an interview.

"Apparently, saying no to powerful, well-connected people has repercussions that carry far beyond the local job market."

She suspected she'd been black-balled.

"You have no nanny experience."

"No, sir, but I routinely handled twenty children at once, more when I worked the academy's summer camp program, and I am a parent used to coping with bed, bath and meal times."

He leaned back in his leather chair, steepling his fingers and pinning her with his unblinking gaze. She looked back hoping—praying—he'd see the truth and willingness to work hard in her eyes. The silent scrutiny stretched interminably until she was as uncomfortable as she'd been that day in the headmaster's office when she'd been unjustly accused.

"For what it's worth, I don't believe your story."

His words settled like a weight on her shoulders. Frustrated because she couldn't prove her innocence, Anna could only stare hopelessly into that uncompromising face as hope left her like a soda going flat. Until the headmaster, her integrity had never been questioned. She'd always been the smart one, the levelheaded and trustworthy one who always got the job done. And now nobody believed her.

If she ever wanted to teach again she'd have to find a way to clear her name. But until then she had to feed and house her son.

"I wanted a more mature woman to look after the boy," Hollister continued. "And you come with a liability in the form of another baby."

"Cody is seventeen months old, only six months older than your son. They should be good company for each other and provide a little social interaction," she insisted but when Hollister's expression turned even more formidable she wished she'd kept her mouth shut.

"One noisy child in the house is bad enough. Two will be a

disaster. I ought to show you the door. But Sarah swears you are the most qualified candidate, and I need a nanny today. You're the only one available."

Anna's hopes started to rise then he stood and leaned forward on his fists, scaring her optimism right back into its hidey-hole. "But I will be watching you, Anna Aronson. One false move and no matter how desperate I am you and your carrot-top kid are out the door. Do I make myself clear?"

Her lungs emptied on a rush of relief and tears pricked the backs of her eyes, because even if he didn't like or trust her, Hollister was giving her the job. "Yes, Mr. Hollister."

"How long will it take you to pack and get back here?"

She quickly regrouped and calculated the travel time…and then the cost. Did she have enough cash in her wallet to cover cab fare to and from the station? Twice. Barely.

"It's an hour's train ride each way and I'll need an hour to pack. We can be back in time for Graham's dinner."

"You don't have a car?"

"No." Not anymore. Public transportation wasn't all that bad if you were careful about which times you traveled.

"I need you to assume your duties sooner. I'll drive you."

That meant being alone with him in her apartment. "But—"

"There is no but. Either you want the job or you don't."

"I do. But I, um…have a question."

"What?" he snapped.

"Mrs. Findley wasn't exactly clear on how long you'd need me. She said 'until Graham's mother returns from an overseas job,' but she didn't specify whether that involved weeks or months."

"She didn't provide the information because we don't have it. This contract is open-ended. You'll be paid monthly whether you work one day of the month or thirty, and you'll be given an additional month's severance pay when the job ends. If you have a problem with that then stop wasting my time."

"No. No, sir. I—that will be fine." Difficult to budget around, but better than nothing. And it explained why the salary offered was so ridiculously high.

"Then sign." He shoved several pages and a pen toward her.

"May I read the contract first?"

"Read during the drive to your place." He rose, came around the desk and loomed over her. She took an involuntary step back. He stood well over six feet and his shoulders stretched twice as broad as hers. A powerful man—not just financially. The same kind who had gotten her fired. "Let's go. Sarah will watch your boy while we collect your belongings."

Alarmed, Anna's gaze shot to the window. She wasn't really keen on leaving Cody with a stranger around so much water. Not only was the property riverfront, the large pool and bubbling hot tub would be an invitation to a little boy who loved to splash. But what choice did she have?

"Do you mind if I say goodbye to Cody and have a word with Mrs. Findley first?"

Her question seemed to irritate him. "Make it quick. I'll get the car. Meet me out front. We'll stop by the drug testing lab on the way to your place. I shouldn't need to tell you that if the test comes back positive or if your references don't check out you'll be fired. No excuses. No severance pay."

"Yessir. I understand. You have nothing to worry about. And thank you, Mr. Hollister, for giving me a chance." She offered her hand. He ignored it. Feeling awkward, she let hers drop to her side.

"Don't make me regret it."

Anna unlocked her door, mentally contrasting her simple home with the luxurious perfectly decorated estate belonging to the man shadowing her like a hovering bird of prey. Her entire apartment would fit into the living room where Mrs.

Findley had conducted the preliminary interview and shared the particulars of the position.

Except for Anna providing directions from the drug testing lab to her apartment, the ride over had been a silent one—and not a comfortable silence either. She had the distinct impression her new boss disapproved of her. And the contract had been confusing. Why would she need to sign a nondisclosure agreement? What went on in the Hollister household that anyone would want to know?

Hollister followed her in, his sharp green and gold flecked eyes taking in her sparse furnishings—a secondhand sofa and table lamp, a red plastic clothes basket holding Cody's toys and a tiny kitchen table with two chairs and a high chair. She didn't have much, but then she and Cody didn't need much. Besides, having less furniture gave Cody more floor space to play.

"Just moving in?" her new boss asked.

"I've been here close to four years."

"Redecorating?"

"No." Many of the students she tutored lived in showcase homes like his, and like him, those families probably had no clue how the less fortunate lived. On the upside, not having a job meant her place was cleaner than it had ever been.

"You're going for the minimalist look?"

"My ex took most of our furniture when he left," she admitted reluctantly. Along with their car, and her trust and her belief in love.

"When was that?"

Inquisitive, wasn't he? But he had a right to be cautious. She'd be living in his house with access to his valuables. She didn't need her minor in art to recognize that any of his original paintings and sculptures would be valued at more than she'd made in a year teaching at the academy.

Just as she had a right, given her recent experience, to

be a little leery of being isolated with a strange, wealthy, influential man. She'd learned the hard way that wealth often led to arrogance, and arrogance to a sense of entitlement. And entitlement led to an inability to accept "no" gracefully.

She deliberately left the door to the hall slightly ajar. "Todd moved out while I was in the hospital giving birth to our son."

"Is that relevant to my job?"

"Yes."

Hollister's eyes narrowed. Something in her tone must have alerted him to the betrayal that still stung when she thought of Todd's rejection of not only of her but their child. It was one thing to get tired of her, but to ignore his own flesh and blood... She hated him for that.

"He didn't tell you he was leaving?"

"No. He dropped me off at the emergency room and said he was going to park the car. He didn't return. I was afraid that— I didn't know he'd moved out until the taxi brought Cody and me home to an empty apartment."

"I take it your husband didn't appreciate you getting pregnant?"

She stiffened. "It takes two to make a baby. Cody was a surprise for both of us. Todd and I were newlyweds, and we'd intended to wait a few years before starting our family, but...things happen."

"What does he think about you applying for a live-in position?"

"He doesn't get a say. He's not a part of our lives."

"Still married?"

"Divorced. Please have a seat, Mr. Hollister. I'll pack as quickly as I can."

"Does he pay child support?"

"No."

"Why not?"

"I don't even know where he is, and if he doesn't want us I'd rather not have any ties."

"There are no custody issues?"

"He relinquished his parental rights as part of the divorce settlement." That he'd been all too happy to do so had killed any tender feelings she might have had for him. "You don't have to worry about Todd showing up at your home and causing a problem. Excuse me."

Anna raced from the room before he could ask more questions. She didn't want to discuss her failed marriage or how badly she'd misjudged her ex-husband. If she wanted to have that conversation all she had to do was call her mother and listen to one of her I-told-you-so rants.

Anna packed Cody's clothes and his favorite stuffed monkey in a duffel bag. Her life would have been much easier if she'd listened when her parents had deemed Todd a freeloader and forbidden her to see him, but at twenty she'd been flush with the freedom of college, overwhelmed by Todd's attention and too naive to see anything but what he had wanted her to see—his mesmerizing charm, his amazing musical talent, and the big dreams he'd spun.

That love-struck blindness had peaked when Todd had convinced her to elope right after graduation. And even though her parents had packed her belongings, set them on their front porch and told her she'd have to live with the consequences of her impulsive behavior when Anna had shared the news of her marriage, she couldn't regret her decision.

If she'd heeded her parents' advice she wouldn't have Cody, and her little angel was worth any pain or sacrifice she had to endure.

The most important thing her parents' and Todd's betrayals had taught her was that she was better off on her own—just her and Cody. She didn't need a man, and Cody was all the family she needed.

She carried the duffel bag and the economy pack of diapers to the den and piled them in the toy basket. She hadn't noticed any toys at Hollister's. But then she hadn't been shown the playroom. Perhaps her new boss insisted on keeping the clutter there.

Hollister indicated the loaded basket. "Is all this going?"

"Yes."

"I'll take it to the car and come back for the rest."

"But it's four flights—"

"I remember."

Of course he did. He'd climbed the stairs since the elevator was broken. Again. The building wasn't bad. It just wasn't all that good either. But it was clean and had been within walking distance of her old job. She knew her neighbors and felt safe here.

"I'll be ready by the time you return."

When he left the apartment tension instantly drained from her. She snatched the stack of bills off the breakfast bar and shoved them into her purse. She had a job that would enable her to pay her bills. For now. And with a good reference from Pierce Hollister maybe she could land another position soon after this one.

She quickly packed her clothing and toiletries into her old suitcase. She'd forgotten to ask how he expected her to dress. She hoped her wardrobe of casual dresses and skorts would suffice.

She headed for the den just as a knock sounded on the door. Elle peeked through the opening. "You got the job?"

"Yes, Elle, I did. I start today."

The thirteen-year-old's narrow shoulders drooped. "I guess you won't need me to babysit then?"

The downside of accepting a live-in position meant Anna

couldn't pay her neighbor to babysit, and Elle's family needed the money. "I'm sure I'll need you when I get back. This is a temporary situation."

"I'm going to miss you and Cody." Elle's lips quivered.

Anna pulled the fragile teen into her arms. "We'll miss you, too."

Anna's new boss returned, stopping abruptly behind the girl and scowling as he took in the scene. "Ready?"

Anna released Elle. "Almost. Elle, this is Mr. Hollister. I'll be taking care of his little boy, Graham."

Hollister's mouth opened then snapped closed as if he were going to speak then changed his mind.

The teen blinked back her tears and sniffed. "N-nice to meet you, sir."

Anna smoothed a hand over Elle's baby-fine hair. "Elle lives next door. Honey, why don't you check my fridge for perishables? Take them to your place. No need to let them spoil here. Oh, and there are a couple of open boxes of cereal and a jar of peanut butter in the cabinet. Grab those and the bread on the counter, too."

Elle shuffled off. Hollister hiked an eyebrow. "You feed the neighbors?"

How did he manage to make that sound like an insult? "She watches Cody for me when I'm tutoring students. With us gone she won't make any money."

"I'm sure she can afford a few missed trips to the mall."

"It's the missed trips to the grocery store I'm worried about," she replied as quietly as possible.

His apparently perpetual frown deepened. When Elle returned with two bags loaded with food he scrutinized her in that same uncomfortable way he had Anna until Elle squirmed and shot a worried glance at Anna.

"You sure you want me to take all this, Miss Anna?"

"Absolutely, Elle. It'll spoil here. And you know I hate waste."

"Do you have a cell phone?" Hollister asked Anna.

"No." Another casualty of her finances.

He pulled his wallet from his back pocket and extracted a business card then a couple of bills. He folded them in quarters and covered them with his card before Anna could make out the denomination. Then he wrote on the back of the white rectangle. "Keep an eye on Ms. Aronson's place while she's gone. You can reach her at this number if any problems arise."

Elle goggled at the money then him then Anna. Anna had to bite her lip to hide her surprise. She nodded, encouraging Elle to take whatever he'd given her. "I'd appreciate it, Elle. I'll try to keep you updated on when Cody and I'll return. Oh. Wait."

She rushed from the room and brought back her windowsill herb garden. "You might as well take this too. The plants will die without water, and you and your sister can experiment with the different flavors when you cook. Be sure to write down any good recipes you concoct for me."

"Sure. That'll be fun."

Hollister nodded toward Cody's high chair. "You'd better bring that."

He followed Elle out of the apartment carrying Anna's remaining luggage. She folded up the lightweight high chair, locked up and trailed him down the stairs.

She stopped beside him on the sidewalk. "That was nice of you. Giving Elle the money and contact information, I mean."

"It was nothing." He closed the trunk on her stuff and stowed the baby chair in the backseat.

"Her father's disabled and—"

"I don't care, nor do I need to know her circumstances."

His cold tone cut like a new scalpel, revealing the armor-plated personality his assistant had mentioned. "Yessir."

For a moment he'd seemed human, compassionate even. But she must have misread him.

She hoped she wasn't making a huge mistake.

Pierce didn't buy Anna's goody-two-shoes act.

He'd taken her home rather than put her on the train not out of generosity, but because he'd wanted her taking over the care of Kat's kid immediately. And he'd wanted insight into the woman who had hoodwinked his usually astute executive assistant.

Sarah had been with him since his father's sudden death had forced Pierce to take the reins of the company seven years ago, and she'd been his father's executive assistant for twenty years before that. No one knew the company like she did, and in all the time they'd worked together he'd never once doubted her intelligence as he did today.

But she was too valuable an employee to lose—especially now at crunch time with thousands of scholarship applications still left to go through and his aggressive agenda for Hollister Ltd. He had a distinct impression she'd have quit if he hadn't hired Aronson.

He glanced at the freckled female with the long auburn hair and even longer legs sitting in his passenger seat. Pretty, but not so much so that she'd drive men wild with lust, and her conservative clothing wasn't going to lead a man to believe she was looking for a lover. Her story didn't add up. And then there was the way she'd studied his artwork as if she knew the value of each piece. The collection was insured. But he'd have to watch her.

Her almost empty apartment and her soap opera sob story about her ex-husband combined with the pile of bills on the counter indicated a woman in dire straights. A woman desperate enough to do things to make a few bucks.

Like proposition a wealthy parent.

Or fence stolen paintings.

He'd been convinced he'd made a mistake in hiring her, then she'd helped the girl, doing so in a manner that made giving handouts look as if the teen was doing Anna a favor by taking them.

Pierce had been surprised when the girl had opened Anna's refrigerator and cabinets because those too had been nearly empty. He hadn't seen a pantry or refrigerator that bare since his stint in foster care.

It was only after Anna's comment about missed groceries that he'd noticed the girl wasn't fashionably thin. She was emaciated. And Anna had given her what little food she had. Sure, Aronson would be eating on his dime in the foreseeable future, but she'd handled the delicate situation with a sensitivity that he couldn't help but respect.

He kept his eyes on the road and the traffic, but his brain waves remained tuned in to the pale and silent woman sitting in the seat beside him.

Sarah might believe that having a woman with Anna's qualifications fall into his lap when he was desperate was a godsend, but if life had taught him anything, it was that when something looked too good to be true, ninety-nine percent of the time it was.

He'd definitely have to keep his eye on Anna Aronson.

Two

Anna's nerves were getting the better of her. Her boss's frowning silence in the driver's seat didn't help.

Without the contract to read or the need to give directions during the car ride back to the estate she had time to think, time to worry about whether moving into a stranger's house—a stranger who thought she was a liar—was the right thing to do for Cody and herself. It made them vulnerable. Much more vulnerable than she'd been in her remote classroom at the far end of the hall at the academy where no one had heard Dan's illicit invitation or his threat to make her regret saying no.

But what choice did she have? It was mid-September and schools had already filled their teacher positions. This had been the only job available for which she was even slightly qualified.

She swallowed, trying and failing to ease the dryness in her mouth. "Does Mrs. Findley—Sarah—live with you?"

"She has stayed at the house for this past week, but tonight she'll go back to her cottage."

"And the housekeeper?"

"Comes in three times a week."

That meant Anna and her boss would be alone—except for the boys—in a house surrounded by luxuriant lawns, dense trees and a six-foot-high stone fence with an electronically controlled iron gate.

Don't be a worrywart. Not every good-looking rich guy is a pervert who wants to play with the help.

Her pep talk did little to ease her disquiet. Something about Pierce Hollister disturbed her. Not in a skulking around in dark corners creepy kind of way, but...well, she didn't really know how or why he agitated her. He just did in an adrenaline-pumping, palms-moistening kind of way.

"Graham favors you," she blurted in an effort to redirect her thoughts.

Hollister shot her an appalled glance which she thought a little odd. "He's not even a year old. You can't tell that."

"Sure you can. He has your nose, chin and hair, and his eyes are shaped like yours even though they're blue instead of hazel. Haven't you noticed the similarities?"

"You're imagining things."

"If you compared your baby pictures to his you'd see what I mean."

Hollister's scowl deepened. "I don't have any baby pictures."

"Your mother probably does."

"My mother is dead."

She winced. *Way to put your foot in your mouth, Anna.* "I'm sorry. Your father then?"

"I was adopted. There are no pictures."

Even adoptive families took photos. But his hadn't? Another strange fact to file away. An awkward silence filled the car. "How old were you when you joined your new family?"

"Eight. And the boy does not look like me."

The boy? Her eyebrows hiked at his phrasing and testy tone. "Sarah said Graham is eleven months old. He's big for his age and really gets around well. When did he start walking?"

"I don't know."

How could he forget such a milestone? Or maybe he was being rude because he didn't want to talk to her. She lapsed into silence, but that lasted less than five minutes before the uneasiness made her ask, "When is his birthday?"

"Next month."

"Well, yes, I gathered that. If you want to have a party, I could help plan something."

"That's his mother's job."

"But…I thought that Graham's mother might not be back by then." She couldn't imagine missing one of Cody's birthdays.

"I am doing everything in my power to make sure she is."

How sweet of him—even if it did mean Anna's job ending sooner. "Well, anyway, if she can't make it, I'll help. Turning one is a pretty big deal. You could videotape it so she wouldn't feel as if she were missing out."

"There will be no party," he snapped in a voice so low and adamant that it sounded more like an animal's threatening growl than human speech.

The Hollister family's dynamics were strange to say the least. The best she could do was figure out the parameters of her role, and to do that she'd need more than the scanty details Sarah Findley had provided.

"Which parts of the day would you like to spend with Graham?"

"None of them."

Anna blinked in surprise. "You won't be joining him for lunch or dinner or anything?"

"I need to work. Having him here has put me behind schedule."

Need to work. Behind schedule. The words could have been straight from the chorus to the song of Anna's life. She, her sister and her mother had eaten most of their meals alone even when her father had been in the house because he'd stayed locked in the library working. She couldn't imagine having a child and not wanting to be a part of that child's development.

She made a conscious effort to relax her jaw muscles. Clenching her teeth guaranteed she'd give herself a tension headache. "I see."

He frowned harder at the disapproval she hadn't quite managed to keep out of her voice. "Apparently Sarah didn't explain the situation to you in a way you can understand. Graham is your responsibility until this job ends. The housekeeper will give you short breaks if absolutely necessary. I expect this to be a short-term position. You are being generously compensated for the overtime. I am on a tight deadline and don't need interruptions."

The hair on her nape prickled. His speech sounded awfully familiar, and for a moment she could have sworn her father had risen from the grave. "You're saying you don't want to spend any time with your son?"

He flinched. "No. Is there a reason for your inquisition, Ms. Aronson?" He bristled a "back off" warning.

"I'm trying to get a feel for Graham's emotional state."

"He's a baby. All he cares about are food, sleep and a clean diaper. I hired you to be his nanny, not his shrink."

"Being one pretty much requires being the other. Since babies can't verbalize their needs—"

"Just keep the damned kids quiet and out of my way. That's

what you're being paid to do. In fact, I'd rather not even know the three of you are in my house."

Taken aback, she stared at him. She'd known the job sounded too good to be true. It looked as if she'd discovered the catch.

"Yessir." For a moment she felt sorry for herself for finding a job that was going to evoke so many bad memories. But most of her sympathy pains were reserved for a little boy who would never understand why his daddy didn't want to spend time with him.

Been there. Done that. And the pain…well, it wasn't something you ever forgot.

Hollister steered his car into his driveway and her questions dried up. The tall iron gates crept open and he passed between the pillars. In the side mirror she watched heavy metal close, sealing off her escape route. Her heart raced faster and her palms dampened.

You're being stupid, Anna. If you'd really thought he was a pervert you never would have taken the job.

But for a woman who loved horror stories and movies about things that went bump in the night the situation had all the makings of a gothic novel. Reclusive millionaire. Secluded mansion. Walled property. Cloudy coastline.

Hollister drove around the cobblestone circular drive and stopped in front of the sprawling gray stone house with white trim. Anna hadn't noticed before, but the house's cool colors and lack of flowers made it unwelcoming. Like its owner. Not that the landscaping wasn't lush and impressive, but it was monochromatic. Green. Like money.

The front door opened and Sarah Findley stepped out, looking a bit harried. She held Cody's hand and carried a red-faced Graham. As soon as Anna stepped from the car her son pulled free and rushed toward her. His little arms lifted and he bounced on the balls of his feet. "Up, Mama. Up."

Anna scooped him up and rose, hugging him close. He smelled of sweaty little boy and sunshine.

Hollister's assistant bypassed her boss and handed Graham straight to Anna, leaving Anna to juggle two warm, wiggly bodies.

"I ordered a second crib and had it installed in the guest suite while you were out, Anna. I also ordered dinner for all of you. It's waiting in the kitchen. I'm off. There's a bubble bath waiting for me." She extended her hand toward her boss. He dropped the keys into her palm.

It seemed a little unusual given Hollister's obvious wealth that he and his assistant were sharing a car. But then so many things were not making sense.

"Mind if we unload before you race off?" A trace of humor warmed Hollister's voice and a crooked smile lifted one corner of his mouth—the first smile Anna had seen from him. Her breath caught. He was quite attractive when he wasn't being a sourpuss and his eyes were actually warm instead of coal hard. But that his affection was aimed toward his assistant instead of his son bothered her. He hadn't even looked at Graham once since their arrival.

Sarah smiled. "I'll even wait until you've put my bags in the trunk."

That's when Anna noticed the suitcases by the base of one of the large porch columns. The assistant's eagerness to leave only increased Anna's anxiety level. What was wrong with this picture?

Sarah turned toward Anna. "I didn't show you your rooms earlier. Why don't you go ahead and check them out. Top of the stairs. Turn left. The nursery and your suite are over the garage."

Anna glanced questioningly at her new boss. He nodded. "I'll bring up your stuff."

"I… Okay, thanks." She took the boys inside. Graham laid

his head on her shoulder and popped his thumb in his mouth. Poor tired puppy. She had no clue of his schedule, but she suspected his naptime wasn't far off.

She set Cody down in the foyer. "Let's go upstairs, baby."

He scampered on all fours up the steps ahead of her. Anna paused on the landing, noting there were no baby gates at the top or the bottom of the stairs. That was a safety hazard that had to be remedied.

Following Sarah's instructions, Anna turned left and located the first room above the four-car garage. The bedroom was beautifully decorated in soothing blues and greens. An original John Singer Sargent seascape hung above the bed's headboard. She wanted to linger over the artwork, but instead focused on the fact that the only sign this was a nursery were the two cribs pushed against the walls and a baby monitor on the dresser. There were no toys and the only other paraphernalia usually associated with babies was a bag of disposable diapers and a box of wipes on the dresser.

She laid the now-sleeping Graham in a crib, checked to make sure his diaper was clean then covered him with a light sheet. Her mind reeled with questions. Why was Graham sleeping in what was clearly a guest room? Why hadn't the house been childproofed? None of the outlets were covered. Who had taken care of the child prior to Anna's hiring? Why was Pierce so cool to his son?

Cody darted through an open door into an attached bathroom. "Bap," he squealed in high-pitched excitement. "Biiiiiig bap."

Anna followed. Cody's eyes were nearly as large as the garden tub which would allow her to bathe both boys simultaneously. "We'll have a bath later. Let's go find mommy's room, Cody."

She herded him down a short hall and through a small sitting area with a television and a gas log fireplace before locating the second bedroom. It had another queen bed, a Frederick Church original above the headboard, and the other half of the baby monitor on the bedside table. She found an additional luxurious bathroom and a walk-in closet bigger than her apartment bedroom through a connecting door.

Again, the space was beautifully decorated, but as sterile as a hotel room—albeit with better art. She heard a car drive away and from the large window overlooking the front yard spotted the Lexus exiting through the gate. Her mouth dried. If her new boss was a womanizing jerk she'd soon find out.

A sound from behind made her jump. Speak of the devil. Hollister deposited her suitcase inside the door and dropped the basket of Cody's things on her bed. His thundercloud expression had returned. "Where's the boy?"

"The boy" again. That really disturbed her. "Graham was sound asleep. I put him in his crib."

"Check on him regularly."

"I will."

Hollister suddenly seemed bigger, broader, and stronger now that he was blocking her path and they were alone in the house save the boys. He seemed to shrink the space, narrowing it down to the two of them—so much so that she could almost forget her inquisitive son.

"Is that the room Graham usually occupies when he visits?"

"He doesn't visit."

Surprised, she blinked. "Ever?"

"No."

"You see him at his mother's?"

"Ms. Aronson, my personal life is none of your business," he all but snapped. "I'll leave you to get settled. Feed yourself and the boys whenever you want."

She had a dozen more questions, the most urgent being where his bedroom was located, but he was already testy, and she was afraid he'd misconstrue her question as interest. "Could we get baby gates for the top and bottom of the stairs?"

"Tell Sarah in the morning. She'll deal with it. Good night."

He pivoted abruptly and left.

Anna wasn't disappointed, but she did feel strangely adrift in this unfamiliar place with no friends or allies.

She said a quick prayer that she wouldn't need either.

The trio already occupying his kitchen brought Pierce to a dead halt in the doorway. Obviously his eight-thousand-square-foot house wasn't big enough for him to avoid his unwanted guests.

Anna glanced up from the banana she was slicing. The last banana. The one he'd planned to eat with his breakfast.

"Good morning, Mr. Hollister."

It had been a good morning. Until now. He'd had a long, head-clearing run then a shower. All he needed before he settled in for his first full day's work since the kid's arrival was food, but the slimy, messy faces of the boys in their high chairs killed his appetite. "You're up early."

"Your son is an early riser."

"Kat's son."

Anna tilted her head, questions filling her eyes. Her reddish-brown hair slid across her shoulders. It was only then that he noticed the strands were slightly disheveled—as if she'd crawled from bed in a hurry and hadn't had time to brush them. That led him to detecting her flushed cheeks and sleepy eyes—half-closed pale blue eyes currently narrowed on him.

"Kat is his mother?"

"Yes."

"I fixed the boys breakfast. I hope you don't mind that we didn't wait for you." She divided the small pieces of fruit between the messy trays, noisily kissed the top of each boy's head, making them laugh, then crossed to the sink to wash her hands.

Her mid-thigh-length khaki skirt and sleeveless top displayed her slender figure and long, pale limbs in a Catholic schoolgirl kind of way. He found her I've-just-been-woken appearance and the faint scent of honeysuckles she left in her wake disturbingly appealing. Warning bells rang in his conscience.

"Help yourself to whatever's in the kitchen."

"About that…" She faced him, pinching her plump bottom lip between straight, white teeth as she dried her hands. "I took inventory of your refrigerator and pantry. There's really not a lot here."

"The cabinets are well-stocked."

"I meant for the boys. Smoked salmon, spicy gourmet sandwich meats, salad and Portobello mushrooms may work for you, but not for them. Toddlers need easier to digest foods. What does Graham like to eat?"

He caught himself watching her pink mouth move and jerked his gaze to hers. "I don't know."

"Does he have any food allergies?"

Irritation replaced unwelcome interest. "I don't know that either. The housekeeper takes care of the shopping. Make a list and give it to her when she comes in later today."

Anna's puzzled expression returned, creasing her freckled brow. "I'll do that. If you're going to join us each morning—and I'm sure Graham would love that—I can prepare enough breakfast for you, too."

Eat with the dirty duo? No thanks. Each child had food smeared on every reachable surface. Even their hair bore traces of whatever gooey substance she'd fed them. The need to escape surged through him, but his growling stomach insisted he tough out this encounter long enough to feed himself.

"I'll fix my own breakfast. Today and every day." And the sooner he did so the sooner he could leave this unappetizing sight behind.

He yanked open the refrigerator and gathered the makings of a sandwich which he hastily slapped together—trying all the while to block out the annoyingly cheerful voice of the woman behind him yakking to the boys.

"Where do you keep Graham's toys?"

Anna's question made him pause mid-chipotle-mayo swipe. "Ask Sarah. She may have bought a few last week."

Silence broken only by the boys' babbling and banging on their trays filled the room.

"Graham is here…legally? Isn't he?" Fear tinged her voice.

Pierce rested his fists on the counter. The last thing he needed was a hysterical woman calling the authorities. Not that he had anything to hide but officials poking around would only slow him down.

Still, Anna believing he'd kidnapped the kid when he'd had to force Kat to list his name on the child's birth certificate just in case of emergencies like this one struck him as ironic. Not that he'd ever expected to be called into duty. Kat had assured him she had foolproof child care set up. She'd been wrong. But no child carrying his blood would end up in the system.

"I am the boy's legal guardian until his mother returns. Sarah has the documentation if you must see it."

"What happened to his previous sitter?"

"She dumped the kid on child services when his mother was… detained."

He'd deliberately neglected to reveal Kat's identity to keep those who might be more interested in Kat's fame than her son's welfare from applying for the job. There had been too many stories in the news lately of employees selling their celebrity employer's secrets to make a quick buck. His and Kat's relationship—however strained it might be—was private. News of it leaking wouldn't help his company's image, which in turn might undermine his goals for Hollister Ltd.

Concern puckered Anna's brow. "Poor Graham. Could we swing by his mom's place and pick up a few things?"

"Kat lives in Atlanta."

"Oh. Too far then. Would you mind if we borrowed some things from the kitchen?"

His irritation reached boiling point. Pierce slapped the top on his sandwich. "I don't care how you entertain the kid. Just do it. And leave me out of it."

Her face blanched, making her freckles stand out. He experienced a sudden craving for cinnamon toast—the way his mother used to make it twenty-something years ago. He used to lick the granules off—

He shook his head to banish the thought. But damned if the nanny's freckles didn't look like cinnamon sprinkled on bread.

"Yessir."

Feeling as if he'd kicked a kitten, he grabbed his plate and a bottle of water and retreated to his office. He'd hired her to deal with the trivial child-care issues. He didn't need her or her sleepy, sexy—no, not sexy—morning eyes condemning him. The kid would be better off if Pierce kept his distance.

He turned on the television to drown out the noise coming from the kitchen and tried to concentrate on CNN while he ate. He had a team of people feeding him regular updates on Kat's situation, but occasionally he heard news on TV before he received a report.

His turkey pastrami and imported Swiss cheese sandwich tasted like cardboard. An identical sandwich yesterday had been delicious. He'd better check the expiration dates on the meat and cheese.

More likely it was the nanny—and her incessant questions—

killing his appetite. He pushed his half-eaten meal to the side of his desk, exhaled then cracked his knuckles, determined to have a productive, interruption-free day.

The sooner he chose the scholarship recipient the sooner he could get back to his real goal of doubling Hollister Ltd.'s net worth before the company's fiftieth anniversary next year. And to do that he needed single-minded dedication and no distractions.

But first the scholarship. He reached into the mail crate filled with unread applications, grabbed one and swiveled his chair to face the three mesh bins on his sideboard. The rejected applications stack towered over the short "maybe" stack. The "yes" bin remained empty. It should only take a few moments to decide into which category the one in his hand would go.

Every year more people needed a hand up. He couldn't afford to help them all, so he searched for the one with the most potential and ambition. The one who'd fought hardest against the greatest odds to achieve the most.

He'd only read the applicant's name when Sarah breezed into the room. "Ahh. My first full night's sleep in a week. I feel human again and well enough to tackle composing the rejection letters. I felt guilty for not staying last night to help with the transition, but with my ulcer acting up, I needed the peace and quiet."

"Not a problem."

She dropped her purse on her smaller desk. "How did Anna and the boys make out last night?"

"I don't know."

"You didn't ask her over breakfast?" she inquired as she grabbed a six-inch stack of applications from the rejection bin.

He nodded toward the sandwich. "I'm eating at my desk."

Sarah's red lips curved downward. "I have never spoken ill of your father before, but—"

"Don't start now."

"But," she continued in a way no other employee would dare, "children are not meant to be dragged out only when it's convenient."

"Spoken from your vast experience."

She winced and her expression turned somber. Pierce experienced a swift stab of regret. He was on a roll of hurting feelings this morning. "I'm sorry. That was uncalled-for."

"But accurate. My husband and I weren't able to have children—a fact that I regret more each day and one that makes me appreciate other people's offspring—in small doses—all the more now that I'm pushing fifty and my friends are enjoying their grandchildren. Graham needs you, Pierce."

She'd passed fifty a while back, but he let her fib go uncorrected. "He has his mother and a nanny you handpicked."

"Don't repeat your father's mistakes. Spend time with your son. If you let him Graham will enrich your life in ways you can't even begin to imagine."

"He's Kat's son."

"Yours and Katherine's. It doesn't matter that Katherine got pregnant behind your back. Graham is still your flesh and blood—as this current custody situation and the exorbitant child support you pay every month attests."

"I'll spend time with him when he's old enough to intern at the company. Like Hank did with me."

Sarah shook her head. "I became Hank's executive assistant while he was still operating Hollister on a shoestring budget. When he began the paperwork to adopt you I had hoped a child would soften his hard edges, but he never changed his ways even after he brought you home.

"He worked just as late and he never took vacations. I tried to tell him children—especially an eight-year-old boy who'd recently lost his family—needed love and attention. And what did that damned fool do? He married a woman thirty years younger even though he was never going to love anyone other than that fickle hussy who'd dumped him and married his brother while Hank was deployed."

Pierce frowned at the reminder. The year he'd turned thirteen he'd come home from school for the summer and been presented with a new "mommy." He'd hoped that they'd be a real family and that he could live at home and attend a local school like a regular kid, but that hadn't been the case. The woman, he couldn't recall her name, hadn't been interested in anything other than shopping and spending Hank's money, and come fall Pierce had been sent back to boarding school. His new "mother" had been gone by the time he returned for Christmas break.

"At least the prenup kept her from robbing him blind."

"You're deliberately missing my point. More than once I asked Hank, 'Why have a child if you're not going to spend time with it?'"

"He needed an heir to keep his lazy, girlfriend-stealing brother from inheriting the company." Pierce could practically hear Hank's raspy voice snarling the words.

"That is not a good reason to bring a child into your home." Sarah shook her head and settled in her chair, piling the papers in front of her.

"Hank needed someone to take a welder's torch to his frozen heart. And you're going to turn into a cantankerous old grouch just like him if you don't let someone past that armor of yours. I understand your distrust of Katherine. She deliberately deceived you. But, Pierce, that's not Graham's fault. And handing out money isn't going to fill your heart the way giving and receiving love does. No matter how many scholarships you award, you can't bring your brother back."

Damn, she had a way of going straight for the jugular. But Sarah didn't know about the baby in Pierce's foster care home—the one who had died. And Pierce had been the last one to see it alive. He pushed the memory away.

"I might be able to prevent another kid from the system from facing the same fate as Sean. That's why we're here sorting through over a thousand applications—with a looming deadline before the announcement and banquet."

"Sean made bad choices after your parents died because he lost the emotional connection to someone who cared enough to guide him. Make sure you don't put your son in the same position."

It was his turn to recoil. Sarah asked too much. Letting Graham—or anyone—into his life meant making himself vulnerable. Everyone he'd loved had died. His parents. His brother. Hank.

Kat would return, and when she did she'd take Graham back to Atlanta. Eventually she'd find someone else willing to give her the ring she craved, and then even if Pierce wanted time with the boy he would play hell trying to get visitation. He'd seen custody battles happen time and time again with friends and employees.

Keeping his emotional distance would be easier in the long run. When he had something to offer Kat's son—like a job at Hollister Ltd., he'd teach Graham the business if the kid was interested. But until then, he wasn't investing himself in a temporary guest.

Three

Four days on the job—two of which Anna hadn't seen any sign of her boss.

The good news: he wasn't trying to take advantage of her and hadn't made even one untoward move. The bad news: he was completely ignoring his son.

Her anger on behalf of the adorable little boy reactivated her dormant resentment toward her son's father and her own. Were all men self-absorbed idiots who procreated without thought of the life they were bringing into the world? Did they never consider the emotional needs of a child before unzipping their pants?

To give Hollister credit, he hadn't spoiled his son with material possessions to make up for his neglect the way her father had. Sure, every request Anna had made had been met almost instantaneously, like her grocery list and the installation of the stair gates and the pool and hot tub alarms. But it wouldn't kill Hollister to drop by the nursery and share a few minutes of his precious time with his son. The best gifts—like love and attention—were free.

She checked the boys again. Cody's pink cheeks confirmed he'd finally succumbed to the nap he'd been fighting. She debated her options. Sitting in the nursery and updating her resume as she'd done during the boys' previous naps didn't appeal. The sun was shining and the temperature was warm but not too humid. She'd love to sit on the patio with a book. But in the rush she hadn't packed any of the books she'd picked up at the swap shop.

Perhaps her boss had something she could read? There was only one way to find out. Dread slithered under her skin. She knew he'd be alone since she'd heard Sarah drive out ten minutes ago, and while Anna wasn't keen on facing the lion in his den, she'd rather do that than stare at the ceiling for two hours. She clipped the baby monitor to her waistband and descended the stairs, heading toward Hollister's office. She knocked on the closed door.

"In," his deep voice rumbled through the wood.

She turned the knob and pushed. Hollister sat behind his desk, a pile of papers in front of him. His white polo shirt accentuated his tanned face, broad shoulders and chest muscles. His frown intimidated her, but she'd come this far, she might as well follow through despite her fluttery pulse and a strong urge to run.

"Hi. I'm sorry to bother you, but do you have any books I could borrow? The boys are napping and I—"

"Make it quick." He pointed at a shelf behind the smaller desk on the opposite side of the room.

"Thanks." She entered the study and his crisp, clean scent filled her nose. She could feel him watching her as she perused the titles—not in a sinister way, but in a way that made her cells tingle.

Most of the books were business related. She was about

to abandon her search when she spotted a hardback thriller by one of her favorite authors. She grabbed it, eager to get started, but paused. "Have you read this yet?"

"No."

"Oh." She started pushing it back into its slot.

"Take it."

"Are you sure?"

He jerked a sharp nod. "I don't have time to read it."

"Okay. Thanks." In a hurry to make her escape, she debated fleeing, but she had a point to make if she could find the courage to voice it.

"I'm enjoying taking care of Graham. He's a sweet little boy and so cuddly. You and his mother must be very proud—"

"Chatting me up is the wrong way to convince me you didn't make overtures to that father at your last job."

Indignation snapped her spine stiff. "I was merely trying to suggest you spare a few moments for your son."

"He is not my son in any way other than biologically."

The odd answer rattled her. "I don't understand."

"You don't need to, Ms. Aronson, and if you value your job you will get out of my office. Now."

When he put it that way… "Yessir."

She turned, in a hurry to get away from the grouch. Her elbow caught on a bin of paperwork on the smaller desk. The basket tipped over, scattering sheets over the desktop and the floor. Some even floated under the furniture.

She winced. *Way to go, Anna.*

"I'm sorry. I'll clean them up." She dropped to her knees and started collecting the pages. Some were neatly typed and paper-clipped in bundles. Others were handwritten on notebook paper and barely legible, their folded top corners all that held them together. But it was the top line on each cover sheet that caught her attention.

The Sean Rivers Memorial Scholarship.

Then she spotted loafers planted in front of her. Loafers attached to long denim-clad legs, a leather belt and a white shirt. Her heart climbed to her throat. Hollister surprised her by squatting and helping rake up the remaining mess. Their fingers collided, and the heat of his touch jolted through her. She snatched her hand back.

What was that? It couldn't be attraction. No way. Not to a workaholic.

Alarm? Yes, that's all it was. A good ol' case of uneasiness. She didn't want to be accused of inviting illicit invitations again.

Her gaze shot to his. Only a narrow span of inches separated them. "You'd think after fifteen years of ballet lessons I'd have a little more grace."

He all but ripped the forms from her hands and stood to tower over her. "Fifteen years and you didn't pursue it?"

"No amount of enthusiasm or determination can overcome a total lack of rhythm. My dance instructor repeatedly encouraged me to find another hobby, but I had my reasons for sticking with it."

He didn't even crack a smile at her self-deprecating tale. She stretched to reach a page far under the desk. Curiosity got the better of her as she rose beside him. "Who is Sean Rivers?"

His perpetual scowl deepened. "My brother."

"It says 'Memorial Scholarship.' Does that mean he's—"

"Dead. Yes." Clipped words, devoid of emotion.

Empathy welled inside her. "I'm sorry for your loss. As much as my sister irritates me sometimes I'd hate to lose her. And…all this?" She indicated the stacks.

"Not that it's any of your business but Hollister Ltd. provides a college scholarship to a deserving student from the foster care system each year."

The foster care system. And he'd been adopted. Had he and his brother spent time in the system?

She scanned the wire baskets and the stacks within reach of his desk. "You personally select the recipient?"

"Yes."

"That's what you've been working on?"

His jaw line went rigid. "Among other things. I do have a company to run. Don't the boys need your attention, Ms. Aronson?"

"They're napping. And I'll hear them when they wake." She indicated the monitor. "But I'll let you get back to work. Thanks for loaning me the book. And please stop by the nursery if you get a chance. Graham would love to spend time with his daddy."

He flinched then his expression turned thundercloud dark. She fled.

But now she knew her boss had at least one redeeming characteristic beneath his armor plating. He was generous to others.

Just not his own son. And that was unforgivable.

"If you're happy and you know it beat your drum," Anna sang to the boys.

Cody and Graham each pounded out his own tempo with a wooden spoon on the copper bottom of a pot borrowed from Hollister's well-equipped kitchen.

The door to the room designated as the nursery burst open, revealing her boss. "What in the hell are you doing?"

The boys fell silent. Graham's bottom lip quivered. He scuttled into Anna's lap and hid his face in her breasts. She wrapped her arms around him. Was he afraid of his father?

"Having music time. Are we disturbing you?"

"Yes." A muscle in Hollister's rock-hard jaw twitched and the veins on his forehead protruded.

"Odie pay," her son warbled, making Anna smile despite the ogre in the room.

"Yes, Cody is playing his drum," she enunciated slowly in an effort to help his budding language development.

Cody banged his pot, drawing Graham out of hiding. Hollister's son clapped his hands and both boys chortled infectiously. The two of them together were so adorable. For a moment Anna thought she saw her boss's expression soften with something like...yearning?

Her son uncharacteristically offered his spoon to Hollister. "Man pay."

Hollister stared, blank-faced.

"Cody is asking if you would like to take a turn with his drum."

The lines bracketing her boss's mouth deepened. "No. Keep it quiet. I'm trying to work."

Another echo from her past. She'd tried so many times as a child to engage her father. "We'll try."

"Don't try. Do it." He pivoted with a military snap of muscles and left the room, dragging the air from Anna's lungs with him. She stared at the empty open door, listening to the retreat of his angry footsteps.

"If you're grumpy and you know it pat your drum," she mumbled under her breath. "Okay, boys, bath time."

Surely Hollister couldn't complain about the boys splashing too loudly. Cody squealed with excitement—an ear-piercing sound that might bring her boss stomping back, then Graham joined in. Anna cringed, but when Hollister didn't barrel back into the room she herded the imps toward the bathroom.

She knelt by the garden tub, stripped the boys down and had them happily paddling in the shallow water within minutes. Keeping an eye on two slippery bathers required unblinking vigilance, but their joy in the experience made it worth her while.

She shampooed Graham's dark hair then Cody's red locks, laughing at their comical expressions. She'd always expected to have children, and definitely more than one. But not before Todd had found a job and they'd built up a nest egg. But life had other plans.

She didn't regret rejecting Todd's knee-jerk suggestion to terminate her pregnancy. She'd thought she'd convinced him they could make their little family work, that if they budgeted carefully, her salary was enough to support the three of them until he sold some of his songs. She'd believed he'd accepted her decision to have Cody.

But time and his disappearance had proven her wrong and her parents right. They'd told her repeatedly that Todd was irresponsible and mooching off her, but she'd been convinced they were only pressuring her to find a man just like her father—the way her sister had—and she'd ignored their warnings.

Using the handheld showerhead Anna rinsed the last of the soap from Cody then Graham. She dried Graham first, set him on the bath mat and handed him one of Cody's rubber bath boats to keep him occupied. "Wait for me to dry Cody, sweetie."

She turned back to her son. Cody splashed and managed to get soap in his eyes. He wailed. Anna rinsed him again. She heard Graham cackle with laughter but the sound had come from outside the bathroom. She whirled around in time to see him bolt through the bedroom door. Her heart kicked wildly. She hoped Hollister had remembered to latch the stair gate.

Snatching up Cody without even bothering with a towel, she raced after her charge. Graham's naked little legs pumped furiously. "Graham. Stop. Graham!"

The little fugitive chugged past the gate—which was closed, thank heaven, down a hall and around a corner to a wing of the house Anna hadn't explored yet. She struggled to hold on to Cody's slippery wet body. Graham disappeared through a set of double open doors. Anna barreled through it right behind him.

Hollister, shirtless, stared aghast at his son then lifted his disapproving gaze to Anna. Anna jerked to a halt.

Her boss's chest looked like a sculpture, the muscles well-defined and encased in tight, tanned skin with a dusting of dark hair across his pectorals. He had a six-pack or an eight-pack or—wow, how many abdominal muscles were there anyway?—above his low-riding jeans. And those muscles were nothing compared to the big ones roping his arms and shoulders.

Anna's pulse pounded like a jackhammer, and tension twisted low in her belly. Her face and body filled with heat. Embarrassment, she assured herself, because she'd just blundered into the man's bedroom.

But she knew better. It might have been almost two years since she'd experienced it, but she recognized the bite of desire. Why now? And why for him, a man whose attitude toward his son infuriated her?

"What in the hell is going on?" Hollister barked, effectively stopping Graham.

"I'm sorry. Graham got away from me after his bath."

Anna's peripheral vision captured the king bed, covered with a black spread. Running shorts and a tank top draped across one corner. The room had white carpet, black glossy furniture, a beautiful stone fireplace and a huge window overlooking the river behind the house.

They'd obviously caught Hollister changing and if they'd arrived a minute later… She gulped and momentarily squeezed her eyes shut. He might have been as naked as the boys. She refocused on her quarry.

"Your little guy is quite the runner. Like father, like son, huh?"

Hollister didn't even crack a smile.

She gulped. "Come on, Graham."

The wide-eyed tot stood frozen, staring up at the glowering man above him. His bottom lip quivered. Anger sparked inside her. A child should not fear his father.

"Graham, let's go get dressed, sweetie," she cajoled, but the tot remained rooted.

"And now the update we've been promising you on the disappearance of international news correspondent Katherine Hersh," a voice said from the huge flat-screen TV hanging on the wall. Hollister's head whipped toward the screen. His body tensed. His jaw clamped granite hard.

Anna backed a step. "We'll just g—"

"Quiet," he barked and Anna stopped much as Graham had earlier.

"We have not been able to ascertain why Hersh was targeted three weeks ago, and none of the extremist groups in the region where her film crew last saw her are claiming responsibility for her abduction. The area where she went missing is known for its civil uprisings over the past decade. If you remember, Hersh's brother was killed within fifty miles of here two years ago while he was covering the coup for a competing network. The rebels have yet to demand a ransom, and even if they do and it's paid there's no guarantee Hersh will be released unharmed. And the longer she's held without hearing from her abductors, the more dire the outcome appears. At the moment we are trying to ascertain if she's still alive."

"She is, damn it," Hollister snarled. Only then did Anna notice the TV remote he held in a white-knuckle grip.

"Hersh has logged many reports from similar volatile locations, and this isn't her first brush with danger. She's one of the savviest correspondents employed by any of the major networks and has often been said to have a sixth sense of impending danger. But if she does, that intuition failed her three weeks ago.

"If the worst-case scenario happens, and all of us in the news community are praying it does not, Katherine will leave behind an infant son."

A picture flashed on the screen of a gorgeous blonde thirty-something woman with bright green eyes holding a dark-haired baby—a baby who looked very much like the one in Anna's care might have looked like a few months ago. Anna's breath stalled in her lungs.

The reporter continued, "We'll keep you updated as the facts come through. But for now we are all watching, waiting and praying for Katherine Hersh's safe release."

The reporter signed out and the screen switched to another setting, another story. Anna's mind raced to assimilate all she knew. She recalled seeing headlines about the reporter going missing, but Anna had been too worried about finding a job and getting behind on her bills to waste time reading about world events she couldn't change. Now she wished she had paid attention.

Katherine Hersh. Working overseas. Taken three weeks ago. Hollister had been taking care of his son for almost two weeks. "Is the Katherine in the story Graham's mother, Kat?"

Hollister turned a blank expression on her. "Yes."

"Graham's mom is Katherine Hersh of the legendary Hersh broadcasting family?"

"Yes."

"Ohmigosh. I grew up watching her father and brother, and I used to watch Katherine's reports all the time when we had cable."

"Need I remind you that you signed a confidentiality agreement?"

"No. I would never share private information unless I believed a child to be in danger, and then the law would supersede any agreement. The reporter said Kat was taken three weeks ago, but you've had Graham less than two. Where was he before you picked him up?"

"Kat had a sitter, but the woman dumped Graham on child services when Kat didn't return as scheduled. She said she wasn't missing her sister's wedding cruise for someone else's child." His disgust came through loud and clear.

The facts of Kat's perilous predicament sank in. "What if...what if Kat's not...okay?"

"She is." He said it with certainty, as if sheer will could make it so.

"But how do you know? Do you have information the reporter doesn't?"

"I have a team on the ground in the region asking questions."

"But what will you do if Kat's not released? If, as the reporter said, the worst-case scenario happens and she doesn't make it home? Who will take care of Graham? Will you step up and become a full-time father?"

Horror flashed across his face, briefly, but she hadn't imagined it. "It won't come to that."

But what if Hollister was wrong?

Anna looked from the stubborn man to his adorable son. Graham deserved more than a father he feared. One who didn't interact with him. A child's mental well-being required more than a roof over his head and food on the table. Children needed guidance from someone they could count on—even when they made mistakes. They needed—deserved—love.

Anna couldn't in good conscience leave this house, this job, without making an effort to ensure that Graham and his cold, detached father bonded in some way. She hadn't been able to make her father or Cody's care. But by God, she would do everything in her power to make Pierce Hollister bond with his son.

It was the least she could do for the little boy who might have already lost his mother.

Four

Pierce stared at the nipple—nanny—in front of him.

Anna's damp and nearly transparent pale pink shirt clung to her breasts. He forced his gaze away from the dusky circle clearly visible through the fabric, but the tight little center point lured him back like a peephole into the girls' locker room shower would a high school freshman.

The sight was damned distracting.

"You're wet." If she noticed the odd tenor of his voice she gave no indication.

"Bath time hazard. These two like to splash. Plus I didn't have time to grab a towel for Cody before I had to sprint after your little streaker." Her lips curved upward. Could she be unaware of the effect of her clothing?

He pushed the button on the remote, silencing the TV, and tried to focus. He had issues to deal with—issues that didn't involve unwelcome guests taking over his house with their exploding noise. He wanted the intruders out of his bedroom.

"Get them out of here before one of them wets my carpet."

"They aren't puppies. But you're right. Neither is potty trained and accidents do happen."

She extended her hand toward Kat's son. "Let's go, Graham."

Graham gurgled and ducked behind Pierce. Grabbing Pierce's jeans in his little fists, he peeked out, his eyes and drool-covered face full of mischief.

Pierce's muscles locked. He didn't dare move for fear of stepping on the tiny bare feet and making the kid cry. Graham's wails, Pierce had learned the hard way on the flight from Atlanta, could raise the dead. Nothing Sarah had tried had soothed the kiddo. He'd howled until he passed out, then he'd cranked up again during the descent. It had been the worst flight of Pierce's life.

"Are you hiding from me?" Anna said in a lyrical voice. The kid chortled harder and danced in place, his excitement undeniable. And yeah. Okay. Cute.

Conflicting emotions tangled inside Pierce. He wanted to get the hell away from the trio. But the simultaneous urge to smile at the boy's antics won out. The kid's hijinks stirred up old memories—memories of playing hide-and-seek with Sean, and racing around the house until their mother forced them to continue their roughhousing in the backyard.

And the nightmare recollection of seeing a tiny baby carried out of his foster home in a body bag.

"I'm going to get you," Anna teased, breaking into the bleak memory. Then grinning in a way that crinkled her nose, she feinted left then right. She dove for Kat's son, her shoulder bumping Pierce's left butt cheek and sending a jolt of electricity through him. The abrupt shift from desolation to desire rocked him.

She scooped up the child. "Gotcha. Gotcha. Gotcha," she chanted as she spun in a circle juggling both wet, squirmy, noisy brats as if there were nothing to it. The boys' laughter echoed off the high ceiling.

He'd rather clutch an armful of venomous snakes.

When she finally stopped turning and looked at Pierce through her lashes, her pale blue eyes sparkled with amusement, inviting him to join the merriment. When he didn't she lowered her gaze then gulped, licked her lips. Her appreciative appraisal slid slowly down his chest.

He flattened his lips, fighting the tendrils of fire licking across his skin. "Go."

But his pulse had the last laugh. It banged against his eardrums the way the boys had been pounding on the pots earlier. Off-tempo and loud. There was something about Anna, something earthy and appealing that he needed to ignore.

She unexpectedly closed the gap between them. "Give Daddy a kiss before we go, Graham."

Pierced flinched, his Pavlovian reaction to the "D" word one he couldn't suppress. That combined with her sudden nearness made his brain too slow to process her words and dodge the little hands that fisted in his chest hair.

Pain hit him like a barrage of tiny needles. His instinctive reaction to pull away proved to be the wrong one. The little bugger held on and made smacking noises with his slobbery mouth. Pierce bowed his back, leaning away from the urchin, trying his best to avoid Graham's wet chin.

"I am not his daddy," Pierce corrected once the pain subsided enough for him to catch his breath.

"Until his mother gets home you're all he has. And it looks like he's okay with that."

Not a comforting thought.

He gently tried to pry the boy's hands open, first from the left, then the right, but the kid's fingers were so tiny he was afraid he'd break one. Frustrated, he abandoned the task. "Make him let go."

Anna's amused expression morphed into one of determination. "Doesn't he smell wonderful? There's nothing like that freshly bathed baby smell."

Until she mentioned it, he hadn't noticed. He'd been too caught up in Anna standing so close as she clutched the kid's bottom half that he could see each individual eyelash, each freckle, each pore, each tiny line in her lips.

Hoping to sever whatever spell she was trying to cast, he cut her a drop-dead glare. "He smells good now, but I don't want to be on the receiving end of the stench this little guy can dish out. He's lethal."

A fact he'd learned from one dirty diaper in the confined space of the Lexus.

Anna's chuckle jangled through him. "Let Daddy go, doodle bug. He wants to go for a run."

The boy ignored her. Graham babbled, drooled and bounced, each movement causing more excruciating tugs. And then he laid his head on Pierce's shoulder and sighed, his breath skimming Pierce's skin. "Da da da."

The memory of another baby in the same trusting position twenty-two years ago rushed forward. Pressure built in Pierce's chest, choking off his air supply. He gasped. "Stop calling me that."

"You of all people should know a child needs to have a sense of belonging. You'll have to hold him if you want me to pry him loose."

Hold him? Pierce had managed to avoid holding Kat's son up to this point. Sarah and the housekeeper had been dealing with the boy.

Bracing himself to endure the experience, he reluctantly wrapped his arms around the kid's bare bottom. Graham snuggled his warm little body closer. Then Pierce registered the kid's weight. He was pretty substantial for such a little thing.

The burden of being responsible for the boy until Kat returned doubled the child's mass. What if the kid got hurt while in his care? What if Graham went to bed one night and didn't wake up like the baby in Pierce's foster care home? His body chilled.

It wouldn't happen. He'd hired Anna to make sure Kat's son stayed safe. "Hurry up."

Anna set down her son, who immediately toddled over to examine Pierce's running shoes.

The tip of her tongue peeked between her teeth while she assessed the situation. Moving even closer, so close that her honeysuckle scent filled his lungs, she slipped a pinkie finger into Graham's clenched fist. Her thumbnail grazed Pierce's flesh. The light touch sent a wave of goose bumps across his skin.

He sucked in a sharp breath as a hot spark of something—arousal, damn it—caused the formation of a different kind of ache as she wiggled her digit between the vice-grip attachment and Pierce's flesh.

Strong little brat, and unwavering in his desire to hold on. The tot's big blue eyes stared up at Pierce as if waiting for... what? He didn't have a clue. And cluelessness wasn't a state he enjoyed. He knew less than nothing about babies and he preferred to keep it that way.

Short of dropping the kid and starting a shriek-fest that would clear a hundred-mile radius like a nuclear warning siren, Pierce was out of options. "Stop. He's only pulling harder."

"Let go of Daddy, Graham," Anna cajoled. When that failed she parked her hands on her hips, then met Pierce's gaze. An "aha" widened her pale eyes, followed by a slow smile that torqued something inside him. "Can I have a hug, sweetie?"

Pierce's heart slammed against his chest. She was looking at him. Was she talking to him?

Kat's son launched at Anna so quickly Pierce almost dropped him. He juggled the boy, and his and Anna's hands and arms ended up bumping and tangling as she tried to catch the child. Her fingertips and forearms brushed Pierce's chest, adding fuel to the embers already smoldering beneath his skin.

Anna ducked her head and backed away. Her cheeks darkened and she aimed her gaze everywhere but at Pierce as she focused on the boy in her arms. If she'd been trying to make advances similar to the ones she'd been accused of in her last position would she practically be tripping over her own feet to get away from him?

She turned and bent over to lift her son, and Pierce found his attention riveted on the appealing view of her behind. She wasn't all that curvy. But she wasn't model thin either. She had shape. A very nice shape.

"You little rascals have certainly had your fun for the day." Holding the two beaming, naked delinquents, she straightened and backed toward the door without pausing until she reached the threshold. "We'll get out of your way. I apologize again for the interruption. I hope you enjoy running as much as our boys enjoyed being AWOL from the nursery."

The "our boys" caught a raw nerve as did the quip about running. Was she calling him a coward? Before he could demand clarification she bolted, leaving him more unsettled than he'd been before he'd decided to work up a sweat to clear his head.

He didn't care what anyone said. With his history he wasn't equipped to be a father. But Anna…Anna was a natural with kids.

He stared after her as she walked down the hall, talking in that singsong voice to the boys. He wasn't the paternal type, and he had a personal rule to never date women with children, so how could he find a woman holding an armload of babies attractive?

But there was no mistaking the cause of his tingling skin

and rapid pulse. He was attracted to the nanny. To her freckled face, long legs, shiny hair and great body. The slight sway of her hips with each step mesmerized him.

He deliberately turned away, shutting off the eye candy feed. He was thirty, not twenty, and mature enough to keep that awareness from going anywhere. A relationship with her would be wrong on many levels even if she didn't have the questionable dismissal in her past.

She was an employee. With a child. And Anna Aronson had "forever" written all over her. Women like her weren't the kind men like him enjoyed then walked away from—the only kind he ever dated. No, a woman like Anna would want a wedding ring and a houseful of babies—neither of which he would ever risk.

Not even if the way she'd been checking out his bare torso earlier had made his skin feel tight. Not even if her touch had burned like an acetylene torch. Not even if her dilated pupils and peachy-pink cheeks said she'd shared the unwelcome awareness.

The nanny was as off-limits as a blasting zone.

With a sigh of disgust Anna dropped the book she'd borrowed from Hollister on the bed. She'd read the same page five times and didn't remember a word of it.

The boys were down for the night but she couldn't sleep. And judging by her lack of verbal retention she was also too antsy to read—surprising since reading was her number one way to unwind.

She tossed the covers aside and paced to the window, but the thin sliver of moon combined with the subtle, almost unnoticeable landscape lighting didn't provide enough of a distraction to keep her thoughts from straying.

Her unexpected trip to her boss's bedroom tonight had been alternately touching, painful and stimulating. She didn't want to think about the latter, so she concentrated on the first two.

Pierce's usually scowling face had run the gamut of emotions from the moment they'd burst uninvited into his room. Shock, bewilderment and fear—none of which she suspected he experienced on a regular basis—had chased across his face interspersed with brief half-smiles that had peeked out like rays of sunshine from dark storm clouds.

His surprise and alarm when Graham had launched at him would have been hilarious except for the fact that Pierce clearly had no idea how to do something as simple as hold his son. That made the incident more tragic than amusing.

But it was his total bewilderment over getting Graham to release him that gave her hope that her mission to bond father and son might succeed. If Pierce truly was the heartless bastard he'd been portraying since her arrival then he wouldn't have hesitated to ruthlessly rip himself free from his son's clutches whether or not he hurt Graham in the process.

Instead Pierce's much larger hands had fumbled tentatively and ineffectively trying to coax his son's tiny tenacious fists open. The beseeching eyes he'd lifted to Anna had tugged her heartstrings so strongly she'd forgotten the basic strategy to lure a child away from something he shouldn't have. Distraction and substitution.

If she'd been smart enough to remember that then maybe she'd be sleeping now instead of feeling restless and twitchy.

But the most unsettling emotion she'd witnessed on Pierce's face had been the white-lined fear bracketing his mouth when Graham had laid his cheek against his daddy's chest.

Pierce's chest.

She didn't need to think about how warm and supple his skin had been beneath her fingertips or how deliciously masculine he'd smelled. Or the goose bumps that had lifted his flesh when she'd inadvertently touched him.

Heat simmered beneath her clothing. Exhaling slowly, she plucked at her shirt and tried to banish the mental image of tanned skin stretched over well-developed muscles, but she only succeeded in sliding the soft fabric across her taut nipples and stirring up more unrest.

If she were honest with herself she'd have to admit that seeing a big, strong man intimidated by a twenty-something-pound baby was both endearing and a turn-on. Pressing a hand over her quickening heart, she turned away from the window.

But what would make a man afraid of his own baby? She was absolutely certain if she had that answer, she'd be able to find a way to breach the father/son gap. Silence echoed around her. The walls didn't offer any answers. And standing here battling insomnia wasn't going to accomplish anything. She thought best when busy. If she couldn't sleep then she might as well be productive by falling back on her second favorite stress-relieving pastime—baking. She pulled on sweatpants, grabbed the baby monitor and headed for the kitchen.

A big, gooey glob of oatmeal cookie dough would be the perfect antidote to her agitation. Just thinking about the yummy batter made her taste buds dance in anticipation.

Stress eating. Never a good idea, Anna.

Okay, she'd try to resist eating any of the cookie dough, but maybe during the process of whipping up a batch of treats for the boys she'd come up with the answer to the dilemma of reeling Hollister in—for his son's sake—but keeping him at a distance—for her own.

Pierce frowned at the application in front of him. The candidate had potential, but something wasn't gelling. He wanted to award the scholarship to someone who wouldn't squander the opportunity Hollister Ltd. provided.

His stomach rumbled, breaking his concentration. He

ignored his hunger and tried to focus, but then an odd smell penetrated his consciousness. Lowering the packet, he inhaled a blend of something familiar and appetizing combined with an unpleasant odor. Something burning?

He checked his watch. Ten. The nanny and the noisemakers had gone upstairs for the night over an hour ago, finally granting him the peace that had drawn him to the secluded property in the first place. No one should be up and about this late making smells: good, bad or otherwise.

He'd have to investigate and while he was up he'd grab a snack so he could work a few more hours. He dropped the application on his desk and followed his nose to the kitchen. When he spotted Anna his heart slammed head-on into his rib cage.

She had her eyes closed, a teaspoon in her mouth and an expression of pure bliss on her face. Dark lashes fanned freckled cheeks. He stopped in the doorway, only then noticing the bowls and pans littering his usually immaculate countertops. So much for peace and solitude.

"What is that smell?"

She jumped guiltily, lowered the utensil and pressed a hand to her chest—a chest covered by an old, overstretched T-shirt that left one shoulder bare.

"You startled me. I think it's the oven. Something must have spilled inside or maybe someone used a strong cleaner and pre-heating burned it off?"

"I don't think the oven's ever been used."

"It's new?"

"I had it installed when I renovated the house."

"And that was…?"

"Three years ago."

Her pale eyes, such an unusual shade, rounded with disbelief. "Three years and you've never cooked in your oven?"

"I'm only here two weeks out of the year, and when I am

I usually order takeout or make sandwiches. If I cook I use the outside grill."

"This is a vacation home?"

"Yes."

"That explains it," she muttered under her breath as she scooped a blob from the bowl with a clean teaspoon and placed it on a pan.

"Explains what?"

She wrinkled her nose and pursed her lips, looking sheepish as she resumed spooning batter onto the pan. "Why the house feels like a hotel. As beautiful as it is, there's very little personal stuff here. But if you can't cook how will you feed Graham if his moth—"

"I never said I couldn't cook—only that I didn't when I was here. And Kat is coming home. Soon. Until she does I'll hire someone—someone like you—to take care of her son." Anna opened her mouth as if to argue. He cut her off because he didn't want to hear her negativity. "What are you doing?"

"Baking cookies. I'm sorry I bothered you. I tried to be quiet."

Baking cookies? Women still did that? "What kind?"

"Oatmeal. It's one of the few recipes I know by heart, and it happens to be Cody's favorite."

His stomach rumbled in recognition. That was the familiar smell, but it had been decades since he'd experienced it. "Mine too. But you could have ordered a box from the bakery in town and not created extra work."

"I don't mind the work. It relaxes me. And nothing tastes as good as homemade."

"If you say so."

"Store bought cookies don't fill the house with that yummy aroma."

"I'll grant you that."

The timer beeped. She opened the oven and extracted

a pan, filling the air with the sweet cinnamony smell. She placed the hot cookies on the center island then slid the next pan containing precisely aligned mounds of dough into the hot appliance and reset the timer.

He couldn't remember the last time he'd had a warm cookie. With his mouth watering in anticipation, he crossed the kitchen and reached for one of the lightly browned, fragrant treats.

"Hey!" She swatted his hand away, and even though the glancing contact was less substantial than the brush of a moth's wing, it burned all the way up his arm.

Damn it. He'd made his mind up that he would not be attracted to the nanny, and he was known for his iron will. Where was it now?

"You'll burn yourself. They're too hot and soft right now to remove from the pan without breaking them. And I still have to frost them."

"You frost your oatmeal cookies?"

"My mother, sister and I always decorated our cookies. It was one of those things we did while we talked about everything and nothing—a bonding experience."

"I'd rather eat them than yap."

She gave him a pitying look. "Sometimes you have to make time to waste time with the people who matter to you. My father never did. The rare times we spoke to him my sister and I had to get to the point in as few words as possible and then get out of his way. That's why I barely mourned him when he died last year. Instead I mourned the fact that I'd never had the close relationship with him that I had always wanted or that I'd hoped Cody would have with his grandfather."

Was she harping on him about Kat's son again?

"You can have cookies tomorrow with the boys. I'll have them ready by then."

"And if I don't want to wait until tomorrow?"

She stared at him, frustration wrinkling her brow, then a resigned expression settled over her face. "It's your house. I can't stop you. But it's also your loss. You will never get back the days you don't spend getting to know your son. Here. See if this will tide you over."

She abruptly shoved the empty mixing bowl across the island between them and offered him a teaspoon coated with gooey dough. "Do you expect me to clean up after you?" he asked. "What am I supposed to do with this?"

"Don't tell me you've never helped bake cookies."

"Not since my moth—" He bit off the confession. His personal life was none of her business. "Not recently."

Sympathy softened her face, indicating she'd guessed what he hadn't said. "Enjoy the cookie dough while I whip up the icing."

He looked at the goo-smeared glass. "The bowl is empty."

She blinked at him, her face a picture of extreme patience. Then she slowly dragged a finger along the inside of the rim—the way he imagined she'd stroke a man. She displayed the dirty digit then stuck it into her mouth and sucked off the batter. The sight of her lips pursed around her finger sent his brain careening down an unwanted path. His pulse accelerated. His temperature spiked.

"Mmm. The best part of making cookies is the stuff left in the bowl."

Determined to focus on something besides the nanny and her mouth, he yanked the dish forward, and using the spoon scraped up some sticky batter then shoved the blob between his lips. The familiar flavor hit his tongue and shattered the barricades caging the memories of making cookies with his mother and brother, of squabbling with Sean over who got the last one, and yes, damn it, begging to lick the mixing bowl and beaters clean.

He'd forgotten. Deliberately.

Thoughts like that only brought pain. A sense of loss welled inside him, and yet contradictorily, the memories simultaneously filled him with warmth. Those had been good days.

He scraped the bowl and ate, keeping an eye on Anna as she dribbled orange juice into a bowl of white powder and whisked. Her quick movements made her breasts jiggle.

Do not look at her breasts.

But he couldn't help himself. He'd bet the corporate jet she wasn't wearing a bra.

What in the hell was wrong with him? The woman had made him regress fifteen years into a hormone overloaded teenager. Was she yanking his chain? Enticing him on purpose? He studied her face, searching for evidence of womanly wiles at work and saw nothing suspicious. She kept her eyes focused on her task, acting as if she were trying to ignore him. He knew she was acting because there was a tension in her shoulders that wasn't there when she was with the boys.

Then she glanced up and caught his scrutiny. Their eyes held and awareness arced between them. Her frantic whisking slowed then stilled. Her gaze slipped to his mouth. She reached across the island then stopped abruptly just shy of touching his face and yanked back her hand. His lips tingled.

"You have…" She indicated a spot just above her upper lip. "You have batter. There."

He lifted a hand.

"No." Her fingers flexed as if she were fighting the urge to do it for him. The fact that she didn't made his nerve endings practically sizzle. Her restraint was far sexier than a woman boldly using any excuse to make contact. "The other side."

He located the errant dough and popped his finger into his mouth. He hadn't intended the action to be sensual, and yet her lips parted, her eyes widened and color blossomed on her cheekbones. She inhaled unsteadily, her breasts rising and falling, her nipples tightening against the thin fabric.

The blush surprised him. He hadn't encountered a woman who blushed in ages. Could Anna's story possibly be true? Had her husband really been such a jerk? Had she not encouraged her student's father?

Tension stretched between them. He lowered his hand to the counter and gripped the edge, overwhelmed by the strangest urge to kiss her. To discover if the taste of cookie dough lingered on her tongue. If her lips were as soft as they appeared. To feel her breasts against his chest.

The air crackled with promise. All he had to do was act on his impulse and round the counter. He took a step forward and so did she. Scant inches separated them.

The timer beeped, making Anna jump and whirl away. She opened the oven door and reached for the hot pan bare-handed.

"Watch it!"

She snatched back her hand, closed her eyes and inhaled slowly, deeply, then retraced her steps and retrieved a pot holder. Keeping her face averted, she dealt with the fresh cookies while he tried to come to terms with the backlash of his ill-timed visit to the kitchen and the illogical hunger Anna had inspired for something besides her baking.

Kissing her would have been a mistake. Anna might possibly be the real deal, but innocent blushes or not, he still had to watch her. She had tricks up her sleeve, a fact proven by the way she offered the cookies like ransom, forcing him to spend time with her—and the boys—if he wanted to collect any of the tantalizing treats.

But the one he really needed to watch was himself. Because apparently he'd lost his mind.

Five

Anna sat on the dock with her feet dangling above water, a mug of coffee in one hand and her second oatmeal cookie in the other. She watched the sunrise and the boats bobbing at other docks, trying to find a strategy to get through the day that wouldn't get her into trouble.

Instead of soothing her, last night's baking had wound her up so tightly she'd barely slept. How had making cookies turned into something akin to foreplay? She didn't have the answer. All she knew was that she'd tossed and turned for hours, angsting over the fact that she'd almost kissed her boss. And he'd almost kissed her. His intent had been as bright and clear as the sun rising on the river's horizon this morning.

She'd nearly hyperventilated when Hollister had looked at her like he wanted to gobble her up. Mainly because—shockingly—for that brief moment she'd wanted him to. She'd wanted to experience the fierce hunger she'd seen in his eyes.

Bad idea, Annabelle.

How could that happen when they didn't even like each other? And why was she so drawn to him? None of it made sense. She shoved the last bite of cookie into her mouth, chewed and swallowed, but the comfort food did nothing to calm her. Instead her less than healthy breakfast sat like a heavy chunk of lead in the pit of her stomach.

If not for the kitchen timer... She shook her head. Hollister already distrusted her and kissing him would have reinforced his doubts. The only way to prove him wrong about her was to keep her lips to herself.

And then what, genius?

And then Kat would come home. Anna would get a good reference and move on to another job. Two bad references or dismissals would pretty much kill her chance of finding employment that didn't require her to ask, "Would you like fries with that?" She couldn't support Cody or afford quality day care for him on minimum wage.

If only she could prove Dan had lied and that the academy had wrongfully dismissed her.... But to do that she'd have to locate the teacher who'd quit before her. Rumor had it Anna's predecessor had had problems with Dan too. But that teacher had vanished. Anna hadn't been able to find any sign of her via internet searches or social media outlets.

And even if she found her, then what? Anna wasn't going to sue or beg for her job back. She just wanted a good reference.

The fine hairs on Anna's neck prickled a warning. She twisted and spotted Hollister coming her way across the lawn. Her already anxious stomach churned like a paddlewheel on a riverboat. She briefly contemplated taking the coward's way out and slipping into the water and hiding beneath the dock until Hollister went back inside. But that would only make him think her crazy in addition to being untrustworthy.

He wore black and white running gear—short shorts and a tank, and dear heavens, he looked amazing. Dark curls dusted his long, tanned, muscled legs and his roped arms and broad shoulders looked packed with solid power. The kind of arms that could snatch a woman close and make her happy to be trapped within them.

Geez. Cork the hormones, Anna, and act as if nothing happened.

Slim chance of that when her pulse skipped irregularly like a pebble flung across the water's surface. "Good morning, Mr. Hollister."

"Where are the cookies?"

She guiltily clutched the bag to her chest. She was determined to do everything she could to entice him to spend time with Graham. His eyes caught the gesture and narrowed.

"Hand them over, Anna."

"Wait and eat with the boys. Please. They snack at nine."

"Wait? Like you did?" he accused.

He had her there. She debated fibbing to cover her stress-induced munchies, but she was a lousy liar. "Umm. Well…"

"Don't even try to lie. The evidence gives you away." He squatted beside her, the strong column of one thigh parallel to her spine and the bent knee of his other leg fencing her in with ninety degrees of sheer maleness. His position put them almost at eye level.

He was close—too close—but before she could move away he lifted his hand. She thought he was reaching for the cookies and tightened her grip. Instead he flicked the corner of her mouth with a fingertip. The sharp edge of a crumb rolled across her skin, but she barely noticed it compared to his touch singeing her like a soldering iron and his thigh mimicking a radiator against her back.

Her breath caught. She grabbed his wrist to push his hand away. Beneath her fingertips his pulse thumped, and hers mirrored each heavy quickening throb.

"You shouldn't…" Her desperate whisper sounded totally unconvincing.

He stilled, and his hazel gaze, a molten mix of green, gold and brown, held hers. Tension encircled them like spirals of smoke, and awareness ignited within her, licking through her limbs in hot tendrils. Her mouth turned desert-dry. A knot formed in her throat and her pulse fluttered like a hummingbird's wings.

Think, Anna. Think. But the only thought running through her head was that no one had ever made her feel this breathless, hot, eager, afraid. And tempted. Oh so tempted to throw caution to the winds. But for Cody's sake, for her sake, she couldn't do that.

"Are you…are you always this impatient when you want something?" she demanded in a wheezy voice.

"No. Never. But you—" He shook his head. "I didn't come out here for this."

The husky rasp of his voice made her shiver. He wasn't talking about the cookies, was he? He meant her. Her, the nerdy brainiac who'd had few friends in school and hadn't even been on her first date until college. She inhaled an unsteady breath. His gaze fell to her lips and his pupils expanded. Then he leaned closer.

Run. But her body refused to obey her frantic order. His mouth covered hers, hard at first then soft and persuasive. Sensations rained down on her like a tropical storm as his warm lips plied hers, dragging a response from deep inside that she didn't want to give but didn't know how to deny.

He cupped the back of her head, his fingers clenching her hair and gently tugging, angling her mouth for better access. She broke the kiss long enough to gasp then his tongue swept into the breach, stroking, enticing, coaxing her to match the slick caress of his flesh with hers, to tangle and taste. And oh, he tasted so good. Like mint, man and coffee. Desire fizzed through her.

Then he lifted his head a few scant inches. The desire burning in his eyes excited and electrified her. And terrified her. She pressed two fingers to her still tingling lips, feeling the residual warmth and moisture. No kiss had ever affected her that intensely.

"I—you shouldn't have done that."

His jaw hardened. "Definitely not."

But he didn't move away and his gaze remained fixed on her mouth as if he were debating repeating his mistake. His body heat enveloped her, melting any resistance. She struggled to hold on to reality. To what was right. And what wasn't.

"This—I—you—we can't happen. You still believe I propositioned my student's father."

His darkening expression doused the lingering passion on his face and worse, confirmed her statement. She scuttled sideways out of reach before he could answer, or heaven forbid, kiss her again, and clamored to her feet. "I have to check on the boys."

"You brought the monitor." He rose beside her and pointed to the item on the dock.

"Yes, well…" She'd forgotten all about that clever little device. She scooped it up and clutched it and the bag of cookies to her chest. She had to get away before she gave into the impulse to lean in to him and kiss him again. "It would be better if I went back inside and we didn't…do this again. Join us at nine if you'd like a cookie."

Then she ran. Like a coward. Like a woman who knew she'd just made a mistake that could cost her the job and the reference she so desperately needed. A mistake that could not be undone or repeated.

No matter how alive his kiss had made her feel. No matter

how much she wanted to relive the entire misbegotten episode and follow it with more of the same.

She could not get involved with her boss. Not if she expected to keep the paychecks coming. Not if she hoped to avoid falling for a workaholic like her father, a man who had issues bonding with his own child.

Because no doubt about it, Pierce Hollister had everything a woman could want. An adorable son. A gorgeous house. A body to die for. And a kiss that lit her up like an Independence Day fireworks display.

And all of it was totally taboo because she wanted more for herself and Cody than a man who would give them every material thing they might desire, but nothing of himself.

A footstep behind Anna made her jump. Inhaling slowly to steady her nerves, she checked the stove's digital clock, knowing what it would read even before she saw the numbers because she'd been checking it every thirty seconds for the past ten minutes.

Nine. Hollister—Pierce—would be joining them. It was difficult to think of him as Hollister now that he'd kissed her.

But when she turned it wasn't her boss. His assistant entered the kitchen. "Good morning, Anna. I heard you'd baked cookies. I've been ordered to deliver a few to the office."

A tangle of dismay and relief tripped Anna's heart. "Hello, Sarah. And yes, I have cookies, but I was hoping P—Mr. Hollister would join Graham for snack time. They need to bond. Just in case…"

"I like the way you think, and I'm in total agreement with you on that one. May I have a cookie—for me then, not him?"

"Of course. Help yourself. May I pour you a cup of coffee?"

"No coffee. As adorable as Graham might be, caring for him last week aggravated my ulcer. I don't have children, and

I had no idea what a monumental learning curve caring for one little boy would be. Now I know why all my friends are mentally and physically exhausted after their grandchildren leave."

"Do you mind if I ask what made you volunteer?"

"I didn't volunteer exactly. It's more like I was along for the ride." Sarah smiled, collected a glass and plate from the cabinets, then poured a glass of water. "Pierce and I come here for two weeks of every year for a working vacation. We read scholarship applications for a few hours each day and then relax at night. On the weekends Pierce has my husband flown in on the Hollister jet.

"When child services called to say they had Graham, Pierce tried to straighten it out via phone calls. When that failed he learned Kat was missing, and he and I dashed to the rescue believing his temporary custody would last at the most a day or two."

She settled at the table near the boys' high chairs, opened the resealable bag of cookies and placed one on her dish.

"Pierce immediately started making inquiries, and he hired the private contractors to go into the region and find out what they could. The more we learned the worse the scenario became. When we realized this situation wasn't going to be a matter of days, I knew I wouldn't be able to handle Graham's care even with the housekeeper's assistance. Inez has children of her own and other houses to clean, so her time's limited. I insisted Pierce hire a nanny. Who knew I could be whipped by a toddler?"

"They are energetic, and when the house isn't child-proofed it makes watching them a don't-blink-or-they're-into-something-dangerous experience."

"So I've learned." Sarah blew kisses at each child then shot Anna a look full of mischief. "Shall we make bets on how long it will take for Pierce to come looking for me and his cookies?"

The blatant manipulation made Anna smile. "I take it you know Mr. Hollister well."

"I've known him since his adoptive father brought him home."

"You mean him and his brother."

Sarah's smile faded. "No, just Pierce. Hank wasn't interested in Sean. At fifteen Sean had too much sass and distrust in a fifty-year-old man who wanted to adopt half-grown children. Pierce was only eight, young enough—malleable enough—to serve Hank's purposes. Pierce was house broken, but not hardheaded or judgmental like Sean. Nothing I could say could convince Hank not to separate the boys. Sean accusing Hank of being a pedophile didn't help my argument," she added with a grimace.

Alarm shot through Anna. "Hank wasn't one, was he?"

"Oh no. Definitely not. He just needed an heir."

How sad. "But if Pierce and his brother didn't grow up together why did Pierce establish the scholarship in Sean's name?"

"I think he feels guilty because he had an easy life after their parents' deaths and his brother didn't. Pierce only spent a few months in foster care. Sean had almost three years. After he was released from the foster care system at eighteen Sean took up with the wrong crowd. A few months later he was killed in a gang-related robbery. The police claim it was a botched gang initiation—Sean's."

Anna pressed a hand over the ache in her chest. "That's awful."

"Eleven years old and Pierce had lost everyone he loved."

"How fortunate he had his adoptive father."

Sarah shook her head. "No one could ever call Hank Hollister a loving father. He sent Pierce off to boarding school as soon as possible, and he employed nannies during every school vacation until Pierce was old enough to interact with man-to-man."

"You mean Hank provided for Pierce materially but not emotionally." Something they had in common.

"Yes, but even then, Hank never spoiled Pierce. He made him work for the company every summer usually doing the dirtiest jobs available. Hank claimed it would not only teach Pierce the business from the ground up, it would build character along with calluses and muscles. As much as I hate to admit it, that part proved true.

"Don't get me wrong. Hank was a good man. But he had a cast iron heart."

Anna didn't need to hear anything else that would make her sympathetic to her boss—anything that would make her think they had something in common or allow her to make excuses for his workaholic ways. She was already good at justifying the poor way some men treated women. She'd learned that from her mother.

Her mother had always defended her husband's neglect by saying he wanted them to have the best of everything, therefore he had to work long hours. Anna had followed suit by excusing Todd's lack of progress by claiming no one had let him get a foot in the door to show off his musical genius but eventually she'd learned it was Todd's fear of rejection that had crippled him.

Pierce stormed into the kitchen, jarring Anna from her unhappy recollections. His angry gaze swept the occupants, landing on Anna last with enough force to knock the air from her lungs. She didn't see any sign that he recalled their shared kiss. At least not fondly. But that was okay. She didn't want to remember either. Unfortunately, her hormones had no memory issues and started dancing in anticipation of a replay.

"Are either of you working today?" he groused.

Anna scrambled to put the lids on the boys' sippy cups and hurried across the room to deliver their milk. If she wanted Pierce and Graham to bond then she had to be strong. She gathered her courage.

She forced herself to face her boss. "I'm glad you decided to join us. I've set a place for you."

He frowned at the plate and glass she'd left for him on the table opposite his son. "I'm not staying."

"It's important to teach the boys that we eat in the kitchen and not other parts of the house unless you want to find half-eaten bits of stuff all over the place. Have a seat."

He stiffened. "I am not—"

Suddenly Lou Rawls's deep voice singing "You'll Never Find…" filled the room. Sarah sprang to her feet. "That's my husband's ringtone. He's probably calling about this weekend. Excuse me."

She ducked out the back door, leaving Pierce and Anna facing off. "Please sit down. May I get you something to drink?"

"Don't."

Anna paused. "Don't get you a drink?"

"Don't try to worm your way into something more permanent than a temporary nanny job."

Anna gasped. "I wasn't. I just—"

"I know how a woman's conniving mind works. More experienced women than you have tried to pin me down. Kat, for example. She deliberately went off the pill and got pregnant behind my back believing she'd get a wedding ring out of me. No one forces my hand. A lesson she learned the hard way."

The revelation explained so much. No wonder he kept saying Graham wasn't his son and kept his distance. "I would never—"

"You've already admitted you got pregnant without your husband's consent."

"I told you that was an accident."

"Who was responsible for birth control in your marriage?"

"I was, but—"

"Exactly."

His bitter accusation was so close to the very words Todd had hurled at her that it stirred her ire. "I got food poisoning from a dish one of my student's parents brought for a class party and couldn't keep food down for days. I missed a few doses of my birth control pills. Is getting sick my fault too?"

"Justify your behavior any way you want. But don't set your sights on me." He stalked out of the kitchen empty-handed.

"You kissed me, remember?" she called after him then winced, instantly regretting the words. Arguing with her boss was not the way to keep this job. But darn it, she'd had it with unjust accusations.

He stopped cold, pivoted with military precision and returned with measured steps until he stood so close she could isolate and identify a hint of lime in his cologne, feel the heat radiating from his body and see the flare of his nostrils with each angry inhalation.

"Can you deny you wanted that kiss as much as I did?"

The unexpected question flustered her and made her wish she could lie convincingly. "No. I can't deny it. But it wasn't wise."

"You're damned right it wasn't. And it won't happen again. I won't be caught in the same trap twice."

Somehow the certainty in his voice wasn't the least bit comforting. He stalked from the room.

Once the sound of his footsteps faded Anna sagged against the counter. Then with a start she remembered her charges. No one had ever made her forget Cody before. But the boys happily munched away on their cookies oblivious of the crazy upheaval Hollister had left in his wake.

Pierce would never trust her. But that was okay. All she needed from him was a paycheck and a reference. She wasn't looking for a husband or a lover, and even if she were, the last thing she wanted was a man filled with suspicion and resentment and a workaholic at that.

The question was how could she break through Pierce's barriers and turn him into the daddy his son deserved now that he'd opened the Pandora's box on her desire?

Damn Anna Aronson and her cookies to hell. Damn her and her freckled nose and the perky swinging ponytail that reminded him of the satin of her hair in his hands. And the taste of her mouth. Especially the sweet taste of her mouth.

The moment he'd spotted her standing in his kitchen, this morning's scene at the dock had come roaring back, launching a tidal wave of unwelcome thoughts.

He'd instantly yearned to sink his fingers into her thick, silky strands again, to tug the restricting band free and feel the contrast between the warmth at her nape and the coolness of the ends and then pull her close and kiss her long, hard and deep, to experience the softness of her lips and the slickness of her tongue.

Oh yeah, he wanted her bad, he admitted with utmost perturbation.

But he wouldn't act on his desires. She was not his kind of woman—the temporary kind. She came with strings—make that chains—of the home, hearth and kid variety. She reeked of permanence, and he'd learned the hard way there was no such thing. Believing otherwise only led to pain and disappointment.

His emotional reaction to her bothered him. He was not an impulsive guy. Logic guided his decisions and actions.

He plotted his path then very deliberately made the chosen outcome happen. Because he took his time with thorough research and preparation, he rarely made mistakes, but when he did, he learned from them and didn't repeat them.

That's why this morning's reckless kiss on the dock had rattled him and why the nearly overpowering urge to kiss her in the kitchen moments ago had shaken him even more. Knowing he shouldn't want her, shouldn't trust her, hadn't been enough to kill his hunger for her.

There was something about her that had slipped past his defenses. It didn't help that her honeysuckle scent permeated his house, lingering long after she'd vacated a room. The sweet smell reminded him of Sean teaching him to pick the blossoms and suck the nectar from the stems—a happy time when all had been right in Pierce's world.

A peal of laughter from the kitchen shattered his concentration as it had done too many times to count. The sound of Anna's talking, singing or laughing at the boys' antics had filled the once silent house making it impossible to maintain his focus.

A growl of disgust rumbled up his throat. Case in point, he'd been holding the application in his hand for ten minutes—minutes he didn't have to waste—and he'd yet to process any of the information. His mental compass kept jerking toward the redhead. He had to find a way to block out the trio and reestablish his agenda.

Sarah returned, a smug smile on her face, a plate of cookies in one hand, a glass of milk in the other. She set both on his desk with a thump. "Happy now?"

"Thank you." Under Sarah's watchful eye he bit into his snack, savoring the sweet taste and chewy texture. He polished off the first cookie, chasing it with cold milk, and conceded Anna had been right. Store bought baked goods couldn't compare to homemade. He lifted the second cookie to his mouth.

"Thank Anna. She insisted I bring them despite your stubborn refusal to sit down with your son. I would have let you go hungry."

Was Anna being considerate or manipulative? Whichever, he didn't need Sarah's disapproving expression to tell him he was acting like an ass. But he and Anna would be alone in the house tonight and every night until Kat returned. He couldn't afford for the nanny to get ideas and wander down the hall and into his room.

Because he might not have the strength to send her away.

The admission wasn't one of which he could be proud. But Hank had taught him that if a man couldn't identify his weaknesses he'd never conquer them.

Appetite gone, Pierce pushed the cookie and plate away.

"What's the news with David?" he asked in an attempt to think of anything besides the nanny.

"He was calling to confirm his arrival time. Sometimes I suspect he's more interested in the flight than he is in spending his weekend here with me since your pilot allows him to co-pilot the company plane, but I'll take him however I can get him. Thank you for allowing that."

"Don't flatter yourself. I'm doing it for me. Once David earns his pilot's license I'll be able to hire him."

"Call it what you want. It's still a nice gesture."

He shrugged off her gratitude. He'd learned long ago that happy employees meant loyal employees and less money spent in training newcomers. But he liked having Sarah around even if she did try to mother—aka smother—him occasionally. And David was a damned good guy. He'd be an asset to the Hollister team.

"But if it gets out that you do such things then your reputation of being as hard as Hank is going to suffer."

He should have known she hadn't finished annoying him. "Have Anna's drug testing results and criminal background check come in?"

"Yes, and as I predicted, she has nothing to hide. I called each of her references—two fellow teachers and the university professor who recommends her to his students who need tutoring. All three gave glowing referrals and said you were lucky to have her."

"She could have asked her friends to lie for her."

Sarah threw up her hands and retreated to her desk. "For a man who can be brilliant, generous and a joy to work for, sometimes you can be denser than a redwood tree, and I just want to shake you. What would you have done if any of the responses had come back negative? It's not as if we haven't exhausted our options."

What indeed? Because as long as he was breathing Pierce would not allow the child to go back into state custody.

Shrieks from outside saved him from having to answer Sarah. Just as well. He didn't have a response. He rose and crossed to the doors overlooking the backyard. Anna raced across the lawn, barefooted, her russet ponytail streaming behind her like a hurricane warning flag.

She played like a child, as if she didn't have a care in the world. Or a guilty conscience. But the wind plastering her blouse against her breasts and her skirt against her thighs proved she was definitely all woman.

The boys followed her like rats behind the Pied Piper—only noisier. Their childish shrieks needled his eardrums.

Anna retrieved the bright blue ball Pierce remembered seeing in the basket he'd carried from her apartment and rolled it toward the children. Her boy chased after it. Kat's son stumbled as he tried to turn and fell face-first into the grass. An ungodly howl erupted the minute the kid lifted his head even though he couldn't possibly get hurt in the thick grass. Pierce winced and every muscle clenched. That eardrum shattering sound brought back bad memories of the flight from Atlanta when nothing had quieted the kid.

Anna scooped Graham into her arms, hugged him and kissed the tip of his nose then lifted him over her head. The wailing instantly morphed into a cackle of laughter that made Pierce's lips twitch. Then she dropped to her knees and rolled with the boy on the lawn. Her son piled on top of them and soon all three were laughing. She cuddled her son with one arm and Kat's with the other, showering both boys with equal attention even though one of them would soon be out of her life—forever.

She should know better than to get attached. But her heart-aches weren't his problem. He shook his head. "What is she doing?"

"What you're paying her to do. Entertaining your son and having a great time of it, if you ask me. She's a natural with the boys. You should join them for a few minutes. The fresh air will do you good."

He recoiled. "We have work to do if you want to spend any time with your husband this weekend."

He yanked the insulated curtains closed and strode to his desk. Unfortunately that didn't completely muffle the clamor from the trio outside. He opened his top drawer, extracted a set of earbuds and shoved them into his ears, then connected them to his iPod and turned up the music.

Kat's son had been loud enough. As he'd predicted, hiring a nanny with a child had only tripled the noise and chaos in his house. But that didn't compare to the turmoil the nanny had stirred in him.

But as Sarah had pointed out, he didn't have a choice except to endure the torture of their company—both mental and physical—and hope that he could control his fresh-out-of-hibernation libido until Kat returned—which couldn't possibly happen soon enough.

Six

Anna jerked awake unsure what had jarred her from dreamland.

She forced her heavy eyelids open and checked the baby monitor, but none of the lights blinked indicating activity in the nursery. No wind rattled the windows. Not even the ceiling fan whirred above the bed.

But she wouldn't be able to sleep until she made sure all was well. She threw back the covers and padded silently down the carpeted hall to the boys' room. A tall shadow loomed over Graham's crib. A man's silhouette. Alarm shot through her and she gasped.

The man turned and the nightlight revealed Pierce's face. Her panic drained like water from the tub only to be replaced with a different kind of worry. What would bring him here when he'd shown no interest thus far?

"Is something wrong?" she whispered.

"No."

It had to be after midnight and yet he still wore the khakis and cotton shirt she'd seen him in earlier in the day. "What are you doing?"

He hesitated so long she thought he wasn't going to respond. "Making sure he's breathing."

She would never have expected that from him. Smiling with empathy, she approached the crib. "I do that too sometimes. Silly, isn't it?"

"No." His face looked strained, but she attributed that to the upward shadows cast by the nightlight combined with the beard stubble darkening his jaw.

She adjusted Graham's sheet then moved Cody's stuffed monkey back within reach. "Both boys are sleeping soundly. We might wake them if we stay here hovering over them, and then they'll want to play. I don't know about you, but I could use a few more hours' sleep."

She turned and left the room hoping he'd take the hint and follow. After a moment he did. She could feel the pull of his proximity like a magnet behind her as she made her way to the sitting area. "Have you checked on Graham other times?"

His expression blanked. "Why do you ask?"

Interesting that he dodged her question. "Because several times I've noticed Graham's blanket or Cody's toy weren't where I'd left them or in a place where the boys were likely to have put them."

"Blankets and toys shouldn't be close to their faces."

Another indirect reply. He seemed to specialize in those. "What makes you say that?"

"SIDS."

This man who wouldn't even share snack time with his son was worried about sudden infant death syndrome? "Graham doesn't have any medical conditions that I should be aware of, does he?"

"Kat has never mentioned anything."

"Then why are you worried about SIDS?"

He shook his head and took a step toward the hall.

"Pierce, do I need to be more vigilant with Graham than usual?" Was that why the pay was so high?

"Forget it. It's nothing," he replied without turning.

"It's kind of hard to forget it since you woke me in the middle of the night checking your son's breathing."

He rolled his shoulders before facing her. "While I was in foster care…a baby died from SIDS. Mike. Cute kid. He was only a few months old."

His grudging confession plucked her heart strings like a master harpist. "What does that baby's passing have to do with Graham?"

"I heard Mike fussing when I got up to get a drink of water. I gave him his teddy bear." He paused, his fists clenching. "He might have asphyxiated in the fur."

Her entire body ached with compassion for him. Suddenly Pierce's emotional distance from his son made perfect sense. This big, strong man wasn't cold or callous. He was afraid. Afraid of hurting his son. Afraid of losing yet another loved one—something his money couldn't replace.

The urge to comfort him, to hug him, nearly overwhelmed her. She curled her fingers and toes and struggled to hold her ground. "You think you caused Mike's death."

"It's possible."

"But unlikely. Graham appears healthy. He has good head and neck control, and should be able to move away if his airway's impeded. He's also old enough to be out of the high risk category."

"But not out of risk all together."

"No. But there are usually other contributing factors to SIDS like having a teenage mother, poor prenatal care, exposure to smoking or low birth weight. Graham's big for his age. I sincerely doubt he was below average when he was born."

"I wouldn't know. I didn't find out Kat had been pregnant until one of her coworkers made a congratulatory announcement on her news channel after Graham's birth. They flashed a picture of Kat and her newborn son. I did the math."

"She never told you?"

"Not until I confronted her."

"You said Kat got pregnant to trap you into marriage. Why wouldn't she tell you if she wanted something from you? It's not logical."

"It is to me. How is it you know so much about SIDS?"

She blinked at the change of subject, but judging by the nerve twitching in his jaw and his formidable expression, she wasn't going to get more out of him even if she pushed. For the sake of keeping the peace between them and possibly getting him to visit the nursery again when his son was awake, she let it go.

"When I realized Cody was all I had I worried about everything, and I read far too many magazine articles on baby and child development and the things that could go wrong. Pierce, it's normal to be scared."

"I'm not scared."

Blatant blustering. How very male of him to refuse to admit feeling fear. She fought an impulse to roll her eyes and shake her head. But in that moment they weren't the nanny and the billionaire or employee and boss. They were the same—parents who worried about their children, who got up in the middle of the night to count breaths and rearrange covers.

Given time she could definitely help him get a handle on his fear—not that worrying about your child ever went away completely. But at the moment he needed comfort she couldn't in good conscience deny.

She laid her hand on his forearm and gave a reassuring squeeze but immediately realized her mistake when his muscles bunched at her touch. Before she could withdraw his heat seeped into her palm then crept up her arm, snaking through her to settle heavily in her lower belly. Her reassuring words vanished. She snatched her hand away and brushed her tingling palm against her thigh, willing the awareness to vamoose, but he must have picked up on her response.

His gaze snapped to hers and held, then slowly descended to her mouth, lingering until her lips felt puffy and dry, before moving down her neck to her breasts. The worry straining his face morphed into something else. Something hot. And sensual. And exhilarating.

Her pulse stuttered, her breath hitched, and her nipples tightened, pushing against their soft cotton cover.

Soft cotton? Her nightshirt. She silently groaned when she realized she'd rushed to the boys' room without getting dressed. He'd think she was trying to flirt. But she hadn't expected to encounter anyone other than the children in this wing of the house at this time of night. Certainly not her boss.

"Anna, go to your room." Pierce's voice rumbled deeper, lower, sexier than she'd ever heard it before. And his eyes… Ohmigoodness his eyes. They seared her.

A shiver raced over her. She couldn't make her feet move, couldn't think beyond the hunger consuming his face. Hunger for her. She couldn't remember any man ever looking at her that ravenously or experiencing this instantaneous and intoxicating reciprocal passion. She was absolutely drunk with it, her head spinning, her knees weakening.

It had been a long time, twenty-two months to be exact, since she and Todd had been intimate. He hadn't touched her once her pregnancy became impossible to ignore. He'd claimed it was because he was afraid intercourse would hurt the baby, but his disappearing act proved otherwise.

Apparently her body had tired of its long hiatus.

"Go now, Anna. Or you won't go alone."

She should go. There was no doubt about what would happen if she stayed. But Pierce needed comfort and she, heaven help her, yearned to experience the intensity his eyes promised for once in her life. And if she didn't want a husband, didn't want a man who'd take her love and dedication for granted and ignore her and any children they might have, then that left only one option.

She could only allow herself short term relationships that never lasted beyond the honeymoon stage—metaphorically, of course, because she had no intention of marrying again.

Moisture flooded her mouth and her heartbeat nearly deafened her. She swallowed. "M-maybe for once I don't want to sleep alone."

His nostrils flared on a sharply drawn breath. "I'm not offering anything beyond tonight."

Could she do it? There was only one way to find out. "I'm not looking for forever."

For several pulse-pounding moments they stood as if locked in time, then he raised his hand and cupped her face. The drag of his thumb from the bridge of her nose across her cheekbone to her temple made the fine hairs on her body rise.

"Your freckles remind me of cinnamon sprinkles."

The thrill of his touch had her so bedazzled it took her a few moments to process his comment. When she did she grimaced. "They make me look like a child."

That hot gaze raked her again and goose bumps chased across her skin. "Trust me, no one is going to mistake you for a child with the light behind you shining through your nightshirt accentuating every very adult curve."

She gasped and tried to look down to see how transparent her old shirt had become, but before she could his fingers plowed into the hair at her nape, and he towed her forward.

One step. Two. The tips of her breasts nudged his chest, firing streamers of desire from her womb. The next step brought her flush against him—the full hard, hot length of him. His arousal branded her belly.

Then his mouth covered hers, capturing her breath, her thoughts, and robbing her of everything except the sensation of his surprisingly soft lips, the hot tip of his tongue, then his slick penetration of her mouth. Warmth flooded her, rushing in to fill every crevice of her body and making her dizzy with desire.

She clutched his torso for balance, the thin fabric of his shirt providing a scant barrier to the taut flesh beneath. But still the barrier was too much. Dredging up a boldness she couldn't remember having displayed in the past, she pushed her breasts up against the solid pylon of his body and matched him kiss for kiss, tangling her tongue with his and tasting him.

He rewarded her by splaying his hands at the base of her spine then ever so slowly he lowered his palms over her hips to cup her bottom and snatch her firmly against the proof of his need. That he could want her so much made her yearn all the more. A moan of approval floated up her throat. She kneaded his waist, caressed his broad back.

One kiss merged into another and another. Every time he lifted his head she gulped air then hungrily met his return. Each exchange became progressively greedier and more frantic than the last until they were almost consuming each other. What had he done to her? This grasping, greedy woman was so not like her.

The sitting room felt like a sauna, her skin steaming beneath her sleep shirt's thin covering. Then he shifted, inserting one thigh between hers and grazing her center. Her temperature rose even higher. A shudder racked her and her knees buckled. His grip tightened, his fingers digging into her flesh to keep her upright. He urged her forward, sliding her sensitive center against him, back, then forward again. Her attire provided no barrier to the tantalizing abrasion from the fabric of his pants.

Her hormones, dormant for so long, trampled all over each other, as she rediscovered what being wanted, needed, felt like. But she had never been needed like this. Pleasure swelled inside her like a helium balloon until she was sure she'd burst from its magnitude.

He lifted his head, his hazel gaze burning into hers and his chest rising and falling heavily. "Do you have condoms?"

A moment of sanity flickered like a candle of common sense. Maybe this wasn't a good idea. Maybe she should call a halt to this crazy out-of-control lust. Because sleeping with the boss was exactly the behavior he'd expected from her from the moment he'd heard the reason she'd been fired from the academy.

But she didn't want to stop. She wanted to see how fierce Pierce's lovemaking could be and if she was woman enough to handle a man as passionate as him. She wanted this, wanted him, even though it wasn't wise.

But...

Her shoulders sagged with frustration, disappointment and defeat. "No, I don't have protection."

The feather-light touch of Pierce's fingertip tracing the drooping collar of Anna's shirt then dipping between her breasts made her nipples pucker. It was almost embarrassing how they shamelessly begged for his caress.

He circled one tip and desire pulsed inside her, addling her thinking, making it hard to remember why the intimacy couldn't continue. Her bewildered brain struggled to put words together to form a question.

"Why do you persist in tormenting me—us—when I've admitted I'm unprepared?"

"Because I am prepared. Come with me," he said in that sexy send-shivers-down-her-spine tone.

"You have…?" She couldn't say it.

"Yes."

Adrenaline fizzed through her. "The boys, the monitor—"

"Trust me, you'll hear them without the monitor." His splayed hand at the base of her spine propelled her toward his room.

Each step along the carpeted hall ratcheted up her tension and quickened her pulse and breaths. But it also gave her time to think. Meaningless sex had never been a part of her past. Because of her eggheadedness she'd skipped that whole sexual experimentation stage that her peers had explored. And that's all tonight would be. Could she live with that? She hesitated in his doorway.

He stepped closer, crowding her until the doorjamb pressed parallel to her spine, and then he lowered his head and seized her mouth again with an ardency that left her reeling.

His hands slid beneath her shirt to grasp her hips, then skimmed upward past her waist, banishing her reservations with a strong rush of desire. Oh yes, she could handle a night of passion in Pierce's arms.

His hands were warm and slightly rough and his touch felt so good rasping across her skin that she wanted to purr like a cat. He paused below her breasts, his thumbs stoking lines of fire in the crease her bra band usually occupied and stirring her so intensely she ached to grab his wrists and show him where she really needed his caress the most.

But she didn't have the nerve. Not yet. Instead she yanked his shirttail free of his pants and found firm, supple, scalding skin. She explored the undulating muscles of his back and traced the bumpy line of his vertebrae.

And then he cupped her breasts and brushed her nipples. Oh yes, like that. Exactly like that. Need twisted through her like a tornado, tugging at every nerve ending, quaking every muscle. Then he eased back. She groaned in disappointment and dug her fingers into his muscles, not wanting to let go. But his strength won out.

He broke her hold and whisked her shirt over her head. And then he stood there. Looking at her. That green-gold-brown gaze singeing over her from head to toe and back again. Her mouth dried. Her heart pounded. And she was embarrassed. Not by her body which she considered okay, but by her underwear of all things.

She wished she'd worn something prettier than panties that had faded over hundreds of washes from pale pink to some nondescript in-between blah shade. A man of Pierce's wealth would be used to luxurious, lacy, sensuous lingerie on his lovers. Not dingy cotton.

And yet she didn't see disappointment on his face. He stared at her the way a starving man would a sumptuous buffet. As if he didn't know where to dive in. His Adam's apple bobbled, his pulse pounded in his neck and the veins rose beneath the skin of his temples.

She had never been wanted—lusted after—like that. Her hormones took another riotous roll through her body, erasing any chance she might have of coming to her senses and calling a halt to the impetuous proceedings. But she assured herself, she wasn't looking for a mate or forever. For now was all she needed.

She reached for the buttons of his shirt. Starting at the top she fumbled them open one by one, baring his museum-worthy chest. When the last gave way she pushed aside the fabric, smoothing her palms across muscles and ridges and man. Oh my.

Pierce sucked in a sharp breath, expanding those wonderful pectorals until the tiny hard tips teased her hypersensitive palms, then he ripped off the garment and tossed it aside.

He yanked her forward, his bare chest slapping against her naked breasts. Heat surged through her, settling into a pulsing pool low in her belly.

His kiss couldn't have been more carnal, more exciting, more arousing. She clung to him, endeavoring to return the pleasure and excitement he imbued in her, but then she got lost in every nuance of his body's textures, the hard, the smooth, the wiry, his stroking hands and tantalizing tongue and all she could do was revel in the hot summer thunderstorm of sensations raining down upon her.

He swept her off her feet and into his arms and stalked across the room. The mattress gave against her back, sandwiching her between hot man and cool bedspread. And then he straightened, leaving her damp lips and overheated skin missing his warmth. He hooked a finger in her panties and dragged them down her legs, leaving her exposed, but the hunger in his eyes as he looked at her while shedding the remainder of his clothing dispelled her concerns about her nakedness.

And then the absolute beauty of his carved form and the thick length of his arousal stole her breath. The finest sculptor couldn't have done better. Her fingers flexed, eager to trace each line, each ropey curve, each vein, each indentation.

He yanked open the bedside table and withdrew protection. She had never been so impatient to have a man in her bed, in her body. He planted a knee on the mattress then braced himself on straight arms above her. His biceps bulged as he slowly lowered until once again they were skin to skin.

"Mmm." Closing her eyes, she savored the feel of him, then realized she'd fisted her hands in the comforter and relocated them to his shoulders. She mapped his shape, dragging her hands along those bunching deltoids and down to his firm buttocks. He felt so good, a tactile feast for her fingers.

He nipped her ear lobe, kissed her neck then a path down

her sternum to the responsive skin of her lower breast. She bowed off the bed, begging for his mouth. Instead, he stretched out beside her. She sighed in disappointment then his lips opened over her puckered nipple. Oh yes. The hot, wet suction of his mouth combined with the whirling of his tongue made her insides squeeze tight.

She smoothed his hair back from his forehead, loving the satiny feel of the strands, and watched as he feasted on her breasts. Watching—so bold, so not in character for her—magnified her pleasure. The touch of his hand on her inner thigh startled her, but his excruciatingly slow upward stroke made her writhe in anticipation. He teased and tormented her, tracing her bikini line and the sensitive seam between leg and body, prolonging her agony by approaching, but not quite reaching, her center.

Nearly delirious with desire, she bit her lip, trying and failing to stymie a whimper, but the pitiful, pleading sound escaped.

"Is this what you want?" He combed his fingers through her curls and brushed across her button once, twice, then he abandoned the magic spot to outline her auburn triangle.

"Please, Pierce."

He smiled at her, a look of pure sexual devilry in his eyes as he delved between her folds and found the proof of her arousal. He held her gaze as his fluid strokes made her muscles strain until they quivered as she edged closer and closer to the release gathering deep inside. As if he read her urgency his deft touch deepened, stroking, plunging, each caress hurdling her toward her goal.

How did he do this? Make her so hot so fast? She'd never—

Orgasm stampeded her, thundering through her body like an out of control mob, racking her with spasms of ecstasy, crushing her lungs and leaving her weak and boneless in the aftermath. She struggled to catch her breath as he donned the condom. Her momentarily slowing heart accelerated again as he moved above her.

Eager, she lifted her hips, inviting him. The thick tip of his penis nudged her dampness, and then he glided in with one smooth thrust, filling her completely. His breath hissed against her temple, his muscles flexed beneath her fingertips, and his heat consumed her. She wanted to hold him there and yet she needed him to move.

As if he'd read her mind he withdrew then plunged deeper, beginning her relentless rise to climax all over again. Each thrust quickened her breaths, her heartbeat and raised her temperature exponentially until her womb contracted over and over and the cry she couldn't contain rent the air. His groan of release followed and then he stilled, only his bellowing chest moving.

Anna melted into the mattress so replete she couldn't have moved if the house caught on fire. How could anything that extraordinary not be addictive? And how could anyone willingly walk away from it?

"I had no idea," she mused aloud.

"No idea about what?"

"That making love could be like that."

He stiffened above her, his expression closing. "You were married."

She wished she'd kept her thoughts to herself. "Yes, but it was never…that…explosive."

He abruptly disconnected from her body and rolled to his side, leaving her with a void she hadn't noticed until now. "Surely you've had other relationships besides your husband?"

"No. Just Todd."

Pierce's face went rigid. She rushed on. "I was a bit of a nerd. I didn't have my first date until college. I think that was why I was so susceptible to Todd's…charm."

He climbed from the bed. "For the record, what just

happened wasn't making love. It was sex. That's it. Don't wrap it in hearts and flowers and don't get used to it. Like I said, I'm not looking for a wife or a ready-made family. Your position here—in my house and in my bed—is temporary."

She knew that. But the words still stung. She wouldn't want to be with a workaholic like him anyway. So why did his brusque dismissal bother her?

The room chilled as a slow realization crept over her. His rejection bothered her because she'd been lying to herself. She'd claimed she didn't want a husband, a family other than her son, or a home. But she did. She wanted to cuddle after sex—making love—and sleep in her lover's arms. She wanted to wake by his side and watch their children grow. She wanted someone to grow old with—someone who would be her friend as well as her lover.

Casual, temporary relationships weren't going to give her that.

She wanted everything Pierce didn't. And she had a sneaking suspicion she might possibly want it with him even though he was totally wrong for her.

Seven

"**I**'m going to take a shower," Pierce said, and stormed from his bedroom—or more appropriately, away from the redhead in his bed.

One lover? And then him. Seriously?

He closed and locked the bathroom door fully conscious that his behavior was several notches below common courtesy. But damn it, a woman whose only previous lover had been a man she'd married was not for him. And why would she have come to his bed if she weren't looking for more—like a wedding ring and a meal ticket for her son?

No matter what she said to the contrary.

It wasn't as if he hadn't previously had women tell him one thing and do another. The first being the foster mother who'd promised she was his family now and that he had a home with her. There'd been several others over the years, culminating with Kat. She'd claimed all she wanted was his baby. Not him. Not her wedding ring. Not his money. He hadn't believed one word of her story—especially since she'd been happily cashing his very large child support checks each month.

And he didn't believe Anna.

He turned on the shower and stepped into the marble cubicle without waiting for the water to warm. The icy spray hit him like sleet pellets, making him suck wind between his gritted teeth. But he forced himself to stay under the stinging spray. Bracing his arms against the wall, he let the cold water wash away every last vestige of Anna's honeysuckle scent.

Having sex with her had been a mistake. His only excuse was that she'd caught him at a weak moment. The phone call earlier in the evening from the head of the team he had contracted to search for Kat had rattled him. The man had claimed he'd heard of a mutilated female body dumped outside the ravaged city, and he was on his way to investigate. The ninety-seven minutes between that initial call and the callback informing Pierce the corpse wasn't Kat had been the longest hours of Pierce's life—longer even than that hellacious flight from Atlanta with Kat's son's deafening howls.

He'd panicked and ended up in the nursery. If Kat died what would happen to her son? As the past few weeks had proven, he wasn't equipped to be a father and didn't want to be one. He couldn't be responsible for such a fragile life.

Kat's father was in no condition to take care of a baby, and since her brother's death two years ago she didn't have any other family. That left Pierce and only Pierce. Father by default.

Pierce adjusted the water temperature to something above frigid and his skin began to thaw. Maybe, as he'd told Sarah, he'd have something to offer the kid when Graham was old enough to work for Hollister Ltd. and they could talk man-to-man. But not before then. He didn't want anyone depending on him if something happened to him. Not Graham. Not Anna.

No matter how good sex with Anna had been, it had been a mistake. A big one. One he had no intention of repeating. There was no point in making more of this than there actually was—physical relief that had been long overdue. As he'd told her, she and both boys were temporary fixtures in his life.

But Anna was a sly one. He didn't know how she'd done it, but she'd slipped past his defenses. He couldn't control his libido around her. That meant he had to keep his distance from Graham's nanny. If he had to pack a lunchbox or strategically time his mealtimes around Anna's absence from the kitchen then that's what he'd do. And he'd do a better job of it than he had before.

His number one goal from tonight forward was to avoid Anna Aronson and to shake off whatever spell she'd cast on him.

Where were they? And what were they doing?

Pierce hadn't seen or heard from Anna and the boys since the middle of Wednesday night—two days ago—when he'd made the mistake of taking Anna to his bed. How was that possible when previously he hadn't been able to escape their racket without his headphones and high volume music?

More importantly, what strategy was Anna employing now? She hadn't tried to lure him into spending time with Graham and hadn't flashed those big blue eyes at him.

Did she think absence would make him yearn for her? If so, she was in for a rude awakening.

He heard approaching footsteps and his pulse quickened, but instead of the nanny Sarah entered the office. One glance at her pale face and pinched mouth and he knew he had a more immediate problem than the nanny's machinations. "You don't look good."

"Why thank you, Pierce, for that charming assessment. And good morning to you too."

Even that phrase lacked her usual sarcastic bite. "Sarah, what's going on?"

"I don't feel bad." Relief coursed through him. "But I don't feel…wonderful either."

Alarm prickled his spine. "Do you need to go back to the cottage and get a couple of extra hours of sleep?"

"We're so far behind schedule we can't afford that. Don't think I can't tell from the rejection pile in my basket every morning that you've been up reading applications well into the middle of every night. I suspect we're going to have to work straight through the weekend if we want to meet this deadline and return to the office on Monday as planned. I even considered calling David and telling him not to bother to fly in, but he's already chartered a sailboat and he's so excited about going out. No reason he can't go even if I'm stuck here."

Pierce hated to interfere with her weekend plans, but he didn't see any way around it. He'd make sure she had extra time off after they cleared their desks. "I'd rather be proactive and lose you for a few hours than a full day. Take the morning off. Get some rest."

"Thank you, but I'll be fine."

For the first time in the seven years she'd been his assistant he didn't believe her, but he recognized that stubborn don't-argue-with-me expression well enough to know when he'd be wasting his breath. She was an adult, old enough to know her limitations.

They weren't even halfway through this year's applications. With the economy in the toilet there had been twice as many requests for assistance. If he and Sarah were going to find the most deserving scholarship recipient before the board meeting and scheduled announcement date, then they had to keep working.

Sarah settled at her desk and soon the only sounds in the office were the tapping of her computer keys. He stared at the application in front of him, but his brain refused to engage. He caught himself straining for sounds from Anna and the boys. Where the hell were they?

Sarah sighed and looked up. "Why don't you go look for them?"

He scowled. "Who?"

"Don't play dumb with me. If you want to know what Anna and the boys are doing go find them."

"You are mistaken if you think I care." But surprisingly, their silence was more of a distraction than their noise.

Sarah snorted in disbelief. "You haven't turned one page in the time I've written two rejection letters."

His ears burned. "I'm trying to decipher this guy's handwriting." Not entirely an untruth.

"I think you're scared."

"Of what?"

"Of letting Graham into your life."

"Don't go senile on me now, Sarah."

"You've lost everyone you've ever loved. Your parents, Sean, Hank and now Kat—"

"I never loved Kat."

"Even if your relationship with Kat was merely a convenience, you liked her enough to keep her around for three years."

"That's because she was out of the country more than in it, and she didn't make demands on my time that interfered with my plans for Hollister Ltd."

"That's a moot point now, isn't it, because of your son. Graham is a part of your life now. Deal with it. Unless you're afraid of a baby."

"I. Am. Not. Afraid," he enunciated through a jaw so tight it could have been welded shut.

"Good, because any investment—whether financial or emotional—comes with risks. I'm beginning to suspect your bravery is limited to the financial sector. You may succeed in doubling the size of Hank's company but at what cost?"

Irritation simmered through him. "Are you trying to get fired?"

She sighed. "No. I'm sorry. I'm out of sorts and I'm taking it out on you. Maybe I should go back to the cottage and take a nap. But I'll be back after lunch."

Concern rippled over him. Even though taking some time off had been his idea, Sarah never took sick days. "Do you want me to find you a local doctor?"

"No. I just need to take something for this headache and lie down until it starts working. Then I'll be back."

He wanted to believe her. "Get some rest. I'll see you when you return."

And that couldn't come soon enough. He needed her here and not only because of the looming deadline. He needed her to run interference between him and Anna, because for the first time in his life, as the other night had proven, he couldn't trust himself.

He reached for his earphones to drown out the silence.

Pierce's office door was closed. And Anna preferred to keep it that way. But she couldn't. Her fingers tightened on the telephone's portable handset.

She'd done everything within her power since that injudicious trip to his bed to keep the boys outside or at least as far away from Pierce as the house would allow while she tried to come to terms with what had happened and figure out how to proceed. The almost empty four-car garage had proven to be a wonderful play area.

Pierce's over-long shower after they'd made lov—*had sex* made it clear he regretted the incident. Well, she did too, because the situation had exemplified her horrible taste in men and ridiculously poor judgment.

First there'd been Todd, who had been the antithesis of her father. Todd had charmed her into his bed with sweet serenades then into wearing his wedding ring and supporting him financially while he "wrote the songs that were going to make them rich."

Then Taylor's dad, who had been married and totally off-limits, and yet she'd been seduced by the nice things he'd said—things she'd desperately needed to hear. She hadn't been turned on sexually and would never have slept with him, but without a doubt, she had been mentally stimulated by his attention.

And now Hollister, who couldn't be more emotionally unavailable despite his sentimental scholarship honoring his deceased brother.

So much for her so-called brilliance.

Luckily Graham had cried out demanding her attention before Pierce's shower had turned off so she hadn't been waiting in the cold bed like a pitiful sap when Pierce emerged.

But plan or no plan, avoiding her boss was no longer an option. Dredging up her courage, she knocked. And waited. No answer. She pounded a little harder. Still nothing.

He had to be here. Sarah had taken the car. Surely Pierce was too mature to act like a schoolboy and pretend he didn't hear her? But then, she didn't know him well enough to predict his behavior. A circumstance she'd be wise to maintain and yet another illustration of how precipitous their little romp had been.

She hammered a third time and when he didn't respond concern replaced irritation. Was he okay? She turned the knob and pushed open the door. When she spotted him looking fit and healthy behind his desk, she didn't know whether her heart banged harder from anger over her knock being ignored or in memory of the way he'd made her body sing the last time they were together. Then she saw the white wires streaming from his ears to the gadget lying beside the mound of papers in front of him and her irritation subsided. At least now she knew he legitimately hadn't heard her.

She entered the room and his head snapped up. Eyes spearing her, he reached up with one hand and yanked the wires. "What?"

His unwelcoming face bore no sign that he recalled the intimacy they'd shared. But her body did. It flushed and dampened and tingled and—

She cleared her throat, hoping it would clear her head. "I'm sorry. I knocked but you didn't hear me."

Waggling the handset, she swallowed. "I wouldn't normally answer your telephone but it kept ringing, and I was afraid it would wake the boys. Someone named David called. He said to tell you Sarah had spiked a fever of 104, and she wouldn't be back today or tomorrow."

Pierce swore, almost inaudibly, but there was no mistaking his displeasure. "Let me talk to him."

"He had to hang up because the doctor came in, but he'll call back if he has any updates. He also mentioned something about it being good he'd come to visit for the weekend because she's in no shape to take care of herself. Should we be worried?"

"David is Sarah's husband. He usually flies in for the weekends when we're here. I'll call and see if they need anything." Pierce rose, grasped the back of his neck and paced toward the window. "We're going to miss the deadline."

"The deadline for choosing the scholarship recipient?"

"Yes." Every tense line of his broad shoulders broadcast his frustration. "The first time since we began the program."

"Can't you just postpone the selection for a week?"

"No. Everything is timed to allow the applicants to notify the colleges of their choice before the schools' admissions deadlines. We always build in extra time, but the boy cost us those days."

"The boy" again. That really bothered her, but she'd decided while sitting alone and naked in Pierce's bed that she needed time to regroup before resuming her efforts to bond father and son. "Isn't there anyone in your corporate office who can pitch in?"

"The only qualified person is holding the fort while Sarah and I are away, and she's responsible for planning the announcement banquet and board meeting. Her plate's full."

"You could hire a temp to help."

"I doubt the employment agency would have someone available at the last minute who was willing to work through the weekend."

The urge to help welled within her. She curled her toes in her shoes and fought it.

Don't do it, Anna. Not if you want to keep your distance from your boss.

But the scholarship was a good cause, one that promoted education, a topic near and dear to her heart, one half of her brain justified.

Not smart, the other hemisphere argued. It would mean working with the man who had amazing sex with her and then walked away as if it meant nothing. His reaction still stung.

But she couldn't help Pierce and Graham bond if one of them stayed locked behind closed doors around the clock. That meant her regrouping time was over even if she didn't have a plan yet.

Resignation settled over her then her pulse kicked up. She had to find a way to make this work to her advantage—to Graham's advantage.

She gulped down her reservations. "How can I help?"

Pierce slowly turned, rejection stamped all over his handsome face. "I read the applications. Sarah types the rejection letters. You can't do that. You have children to watch."

"No, I can't stay tied to a desk typing, but I can read applications while the boys are sleeping, and probably even while they're awake. Children this age play independently. All they need is supervision."

"Not a good idea."

"I agree that our working together might not be the best course of action, but do you really have alternatives?"

"I choose the winner. You don't know what I'm looking for."

"Pierce—Mr. Hollister, I'm a teacher. You're looking for a student—a special student, possibly an exceptional one. One with potential. Qualities I can identify. Maybe I can't choose your winner, but I can at least weed out the undesirables and decrease the number of applications you have to read."

His shoulders remained rigid. His jaw shifted left, right, like a pendulum. She pushed her advantage. "Would you rather accept failure as inevitable or rally against it and at least have a chance at success?"

He looked as if working with her was about as palatable as a plate of worms. She shrugged. "My offer's on the table. If you change your mind you know where to find me."

She had taken only three steps toward the kitchen when he called her name. She paused without turning, her heart slamming wildly against her breast bone.

"I could use your help."

Adrenaline pulsed through her veins, making her extremities tingle.

"But only for this project," he continued in a frigid tone that practically gave her frostbite. "This had better not be some thinly veiled strategy to get back into my bed."

She hoped he couldn't see her flinch from behind. For a moment she contemplated ignoring him and letting him suffer for his arrogance. But for Graham's sake, she couldn't. She swung around but wisely bit her tongue until she had control of her hurt, anger and stinging pride. She'd learned from her father that irate outbursts never solved anything. She had to utilize strategy and reason.

"It isn't. We both know our…intimate encounter was a mistake. Tell me what you'd like me to do."

"We need to focus on selection. The rejection letters will have to wait. As you said, you can discard the obviously unqualified and pass any potential winners on to me." He tapped a few keys then stood and motioned for her to take his seat. "This is our web page describing our ideal candidate."

Anna circled his desk and sank into his chair. The leather retained his body heat and scent, leaving her with a feeling of being enfolded by him, which reawakened all kinds of memories—sensual memories she'd rather keep snoozing. It didn't help when he leaned over her bracing one hand beside her on the desk and the other on the back of the chair. He was close. Too close.

Awareness blossomed inside her and no matter how hard she tried she could not stem her reaction. She blinked, licked dry lips and tried to focus on her breathing, but that only filled her lungs with his subtle cologne.

She stared hard at the screen. It took a few moments for the hormonal dust to settle and the text to make sense. When she finished reading she leaned back, aiming to put as much distance between them as she could. The angle left her gazing up at his chin and the stubble already darkening his jaw. Encircling his mouth.

She instantly recalled the erotic prickle of those bristles against her tender skin and how soft his lips had been in contrast. Digging her short nails into the chair's armrests, she fought the mental images forming in her brain of him at her breast suckling, rasping her with that chin.

Then she made the mistake of looking into his eyes, and as if she'd telegraphed her torrid thoughts, his pupils expanded. His nostrils flared, pinching white with each breath. A muscle bunched in his jaw then his Adam's apple bobbed as he swallowed.

Reciprocal desire simmered low in her abdomen. So much for being smart and strong and resisting temptation. She averted her gaze and cleared her throat. She would not give in again. Once had taught her a hard lesson. Twice would be torture.

"I have a pretty good idea of what you want. In a scholarship recipient," she added hastily when his chest expanded rapidly. "You're looking for someone who hasn't let adversity defeat him or her, someone who hasn't quit trying just because the odds are stacked overwhelmingly against him. A candidate who isn't looking for shortcuts or the easiest route. Someone who wants a hand up, not a hand out."

"I should have had you write the press release." The surprise and approval in his voice filled her with warmth. She made the mistake of linking her gaze to his again. The memory of that night loomed like a living being between them, connecting them in a way that was both palpable and strong. And wrong.

Her lungs refused to let air in or out, and the longer their eyes held the tighter the rope of desire twisted in her middle. But for him sex was like scratching an itch, and she'd learned from their encounter that it was more than that for her.

So maybe she needed just a teensy bit longer to get a handle on this situation.

She abruptly shoved the chair back, forcing him to move or risk getting his feet run over, then she ordered her shaking legs to carry her to the opposite side of the desk and as far away as the room would allow.

"I'd like to review a few of the rejected applications first then some of the maybes just to see if I can pinpoint the spark that sets them apart."

"Help yourself. Take a stack to the nursery with you."

Tempting, but not reasonable. "It would be best if I read them in here in case I have questions."

His scowl made it clear he didn't want her nearby. How did he turn off the hunger so easily?

"Only until I get the hang of it. Then I will happily work as far away from you as I possibly can." Oops. That hadn't sounded nice.

"That would be for the best, Anna."

"This has to be a mistake."

Anna's voice shattered Pierce's concentration—not for the first time—making him realize he'd been fixated not on the application in his hand but on the long lock of hair she'd been coiling around her finger as she read. He'd been visualizing the satiny russet strands winding around something else— something they hadn't gotten around to the other night.

A part of his anatomy growing harder and hotter by the second at the thought of her hair—her tongue—twining around him.

He trampled the thought. "What is a mistake?"

"This candidate shouldn't have been rejected."

"Let me see."

She unfolded the legs she'd tucked beneath her in the leather chair facing his desk—the legs she had yet to wind around him—and rolled to her feet with a graceful fluidity that hinted of the dance classes she'd mentioned. As she approached his desk, papers in hand, her honeysuckle fragrance encroached into his space. That same scent lingered on his sheets. He needed to demand the housekeeper change them. Today. And then maybe he would sleep tonight instead of tossing and turning with illicit dreams.

Damn that night that should never have happened. It had activated some primal hunter's instinct in him that he couldn't put to rest. His mind kept drifting to what he and Anna had done. And what he still yearned to do with her.

Irritated with himself for his loss of focus, he snatched the pages from her and skimmed the typed words, quickly finding the reason this guy was a reject. "He's an underachiever."

"He has a 4.0 average and an incredibly high score on the SAT. He's been active in several community groups and has acted as a peer tutor since he turned fourteen. And he's the school mascot."

"Look at his career choice."

"He wants to be a high school counselor. What's wrong with that?"

Annoyed with her for arguing over a non-issue and even more so with himself because of his fascination with her, he stabbed the papers back at her. "We're looking for someone with more ambition."

"Are you saying he's less deserving because he chooses to define success on a more personal and less lucrative level? Not everyone yearns to be the CEO of a Fortune 500 company."

"Anna, do you know this boy?"

"No, but—"

"Then why are you arguing over a kid you've never met?"

She stared at the cover sheet then the floor, color climbing her cheeks. Then she did that thing—the one she often did when nervous. She shifted her feet. Did she have any idea how erotic the sight of her thighs rubbing together was to him?

"He reminds me of me," she replied without lifting her head.

This ought to be good. What did a kid with seven years in the system have in common with a pampered Vanderbilt graduate? Leaning back, he folded his arms. "In what way is he like you?"

"He is president of the science and debate clubs and class valedictorian. Translation: an egghead. You were probably a jock so you wouldn't know how miserable high school can be for us geeky types."

He didn't bother to confirm her statement. Instead he tried to visualize Anna as a gawky teen and couldn't. Not with those subtle curves, her thick and glossy auburn hair, creamy, cinnamon-sprinkled skin and those incredible eyes. How could any guy overlook that combination?

"I would have pictured you as a cheerleader, class president or homecoming queen."

She shook her head and her hair slid over her shoulder—the way he wanted the strands to glide across his skin. "That was my sister. But I learned to make my disadvantages work for me."

That caught his attention. "Work for you how?"

"I was smart enough to connect with the jocks, cheerleaders and popular students through tutoring them. And those ballet classes I mentioned, I took them even though I was a total klutz because the lessons gave several of the popular girls an opportunity to mentor me. The tutor/tutee reversal acted as an equalizer and kept me from being a social pariah. The girls didn't become my friends, but they became allies of a sort so I didn't get picked on or bullied. This young man's doing the same. It's smart. Strategic. Don't underestimate him."

Strategic indeed. He'd have to keep that in mind. He might have underestimated Anna's cunning. "Even if he is successful it will be on a small scale. Barely a ripple in the pond of life. Why should I waste Hollister Ltd.'s funds on him when I can finance someone who'll have a larger impact?"

"Counselors and teachers have a more pervasive influence than you know. They guide their students through difficult situations that could undermine their success in school. Success in school can translate into success in other parts of their lives. A good teacher or counselor ensures that children under her umbrella feel safe and appreciated. She'll teach them their opinions have value and allow them to voice their thoughts without fear of reprisal or ridicule. Not every child is given that simple courtesy at home."

The passionate flush on her cheeks told him she honestly believed the crap rolling off her tongue. And he'd obviously hit one of her hot buttons. Not the same one he'd hit two nights ago.

He blinked, trying to banish the image of her flushed face while he'd stroked that button. "I take it you weren't given that courtesy."

Her legs swished again, distracting him once more. Damn it.

"My father was the only one allowed to have opinions in our house. My mother never made a decision without consulting him first. She, my older sister and I were expected to do as daddy ordered—right down to choosing our future careers—instead of thinking for ourselves and making our own choices. Unless you want a bunch of inept followers and no leaders that is not the way to prepare the next generation."

Hank had been the same way. Barking orders. Never taking no for an answer. Not accepting failure on any level. Pierce had learned to let Hank have his say, then Pierce had gone his own way. "Your father told you to become a teacher?"

"No. He insisted I major in art history so I'd be an asset to my future husband."

"But you didn't."

"I minored in art, but I wanted to teach, so I majored in education. He was livid when he read my diploma."

"He didn't find out until after you'd graduated?"

"He didn't care enough to ask."

The nanny had backbone. He'd admire that in another woman, but right now he did not need her telling him how to spend his money. "Your education is why you stare at my paintings."

"Not stare. Study. Admire. I haven't seen originals by these artists outside books and museums."

"They're an investment."

"An investment that stays locked away in a vacation home where they are rarely appreciated."

"Are you lecturing me, Anna?"

"Your collection includes some of America's finest artists. It's a shame not to share. You could loan them to a museum and not devalue your investment."

Was she trying to make him feel selfish? Or trying to distract him from the task at hand? Or trying to swindle him out of his artwork?

"And I suppose you want to arrange that for me?"

"Good heavens no. I don't have those kinds of connections. But I can help you make them."

Interesting approach. Step back. Lure him into a false sense of security. No dice.

"This candidate is not our man," he stated with a finality that should have had her slinking back to her seat in defeat. He took the application from her hand and tossed it back into the "no" stack.

"You should give him a chance."

"Counselors didn't help my brother. Sean went from being a straight-A student to a failing one in the six months before we were separated. No one—least of all his school counselor—bothered to ask why."

Sympathy softened her eyes. "It wasn't just grief over losing your parents?"

"No. We were assigned so many chores in our foster home that he didn't have time to study. Hell, he barely had time to sleep and we were scarcely given enough to eat."

A baby's cry erupted from the monitor, but this time,

instead of warping Pierce's nerves with tension, the racket filled him with relief—the opposite reaction to each of the previous times he'd heard the noise.

He wanted to stop thinking about Anna, about how he had barely scratched the surface of the intense hunger she aroused in him and the combustible chemistry they shared. Hell, he hadn't even tasted the sweetness between her legs or felt the warmth of her mouth around his penis. If she left the study maybe he could concentrate on the candidates instead of sex.

Anna crossed to the bin, picked up the rejected application and deliberately moved it to the "yes" basket. He almost laughed at her audacity. "At least interview him."

"Go," he ordered, eager to have his office, his sanctuary and his solitude back. The minute she left the room he moved the file back to the rejects then paused with his hand in midair.

Her arguments were valid, and yes, his personal bias against counselors might have had something to do with rejecting the kid.

Pierce could almost admire Anna for supporting the underdog. If someone had felt as strongly for Sean his brother would never have slipped through the cracks and there would be no need for this memorial scholarship. But the system had failed.

And liking and respecting Anna's opinion or anything else about her was definitely not part of his plan. He needed her to watch Kat's son, and as soon as Kat returned Anna and her boy would be gone. Forgotten. Like every other lover from his past.

But he had learned something vital from their time-wasting chat. Anna knew how to use and manipulate people to her advantage. The poor suckers in her high school probably never knew what had hit them.

He would not be as gullible.

Eight

Anna's zombielike exhaustion vaporized the instant Pierce strode into his office Saturday morning making the air—and her—crackle with energy.

He'd yet to notice her sitting on the floor with her back to the French doors or Graham sleeping on a blanket by her side with his little rump stuck up in the air and his thumb tucked into his rosebud mouth.

Pierce circled his desk and sat down. He clicked on his desk lamp. She knew the exact second he realized he wasn't alone because he froze mid-reach to his computer's power switch. His gaze snapped in her direction. "What are you doing there?"

She put a finger to her lips then pointed at the precious pink-cheeked mound beside her. "Graham was fussy. Probably teething," she whispered. "I brought him downstairs so he wouldn't disturb you and Cody, and I thought I might as well be productive since I'm awake. The patio's outside lighting provides enough illumination for me to read without turning on a lamp."

She indicated the two stacks of applications on the floor nearby with the one in her hand.

"Take him back to the nursery." His husky whisper gave her goose bumps. It reminded her of late night conversations. In the dark. After sex.

Do not think about sex, Annabelle.

But her boss's lean, muscled body, deliciously clad in thigh-hugging jeans and a black T-shirt, and his freshly shaven jaw stirred her hormones into frenzy.

How could the attraction be so strong and so wrong?

"I can't move Graham without waking him, and he needs his sleep."

His astute hazel gaze raked over her. "Judging by the shadows beneath your eyes, so do you. Did he keep you up all night?"

Surprised by his softly voiced query, she shrugged. "I slept when he did."

But then the granite expression returned. "I can't work with him in the room."

"The longer he sleeps the more applications I can get through. I'll take him away the minute he wakes."

Pierce didn't look happy about that, then his attention shifted to the small table beside her. "Cookies for breakfast again?"

She grimaced. "Bad habit."

"Is that coffee?"

"I made it about an hour ago. There's more in the kitchen. If you'll stay with Graham I'll refill my cup and bring you one."

"No." His sharp response made the baby squirm and whimper.

Anna patted Graham's back until he settled.

Pierce rose. "I'll refill your cup when I get mine."

He crossed the room to retrieve her mug. When he lifted the mug but didn't move away she looked up and caught his gaze fixed on her chest. Hers followed. She groaned silently, wanting to disappear when she saw the neckline of her camisole gaping open to reveal the tops of her breasts and her erect nipples.

She'd worn this as sleeping attire because it covered more than her nightshirt and didn't remind her of the other night, but that didn't account for him standing over her.

Why had she forgotten to pack a robe?

She had hustled downstairs in the wee hours of the morning to avoid waking her boss and having him complain about Graham's crying, and she hadn't expected company at 5:00 a.m. given how late Pierce had been staying up. And that of course was how the other night had started...

She rested the application in her hand against her chest. But it was too late. Pierce's passion-darkened eyes said he'd already gotten an eyeful of her unintentional display.

"Get dressed. He'll be fine until you get back."

She didn't argue. Instead, she slowly stood, which put her so close to Pierce she could smell his minty toothpaste. An almost visceral need to stroke his smooth jaw swept through her, but she restrained the urge by clenching her fists by her side. Awareness formed an odd tension between them.

"Anna. Go. Get. Dressed." His voice rumbled like distant thunder. It was small comfort to know he felt it too—this compulsion that they both knew was wrong, pointless and a dead end. And even if their expectations weren't poles apart, he was an emotionally unavailable workaholic. A double negative, in her opinion.

She struggled to recall the reason she'd risen. Escape. No, clothes. "If he fusses just rub his back."

He looked as if the idea horrified him. "You have five minutes."

Five minutes. Anna fled the room, the man and the sexual urges turning her body into a stranger's and raced up the stairs, detouring by the nursery. She paused to count Cody's breaths—something she'd done every night since bringing him home and realizing she was solely responsible for his welfare.

When she was satisfied he was well, she dashed into her room and yanked on jeans and a long-sleeved knit shirt. The outfit was probably too casual, but these were the most concealing garments she'd packed. The last thing she needed was to reinforce Pierce's belief that she was trying to be provocative.

She took scant time for hygiene basics before heading for the stairs. Cody's morning babble stopped her on the second tread. She backtracked to the nursery. His face lit up when he saw her, making her heart flood with joy.

"Good morning, handsome." She gave him a big, noisy kiss on his cheek. "I love you."

"Mama." He patted his diaper. "Odie wet."

A sure sign potty training wasn't far away. "Let's get you a dry diaper then we'll have breakfast."

"Hungee."

"You are always hungry, young man." She sang his favorite song while she took care of business then scooped him up, hugged him close and headed downstairs.

Graham's cries carried all the way into the foyer. Anna quickened her step, but then she heard Pierce's voice. "Don't cry, kid. She'll be right down. Here, eat this."

Curious as to what Pierce was feeding his child, she slowed her steps and paused outside the office. Pierce sat at his desk with Graham standing by his knee. He awkwardly patted his son's back with one hand and offered the teary eyed tot one of Anna's cookies with the other. It was shocking to see how tentative those long-fingered hands were now. The other night they had moved over her body with confidence and skill creating magic and— Stop.

Graham lifted his little arms, asking to be held. "Da da da."

Anna silently willed Pierce to pick up his son.

"I'm not your da da, okay? I'm not. I can't be."

Can't be? How could Pierce resist his adorable baby? How could he not love Graham? But there was no sign of tenderness in his face. Only fear. She recognized it now that she knew what to look for.

She debated giving them a few more minutes to see if Pierce would give into his son's plea, but she'd already missed her five minute deadline thanks to Cody's diaper. She stepped into the room.

Pierce's jaw snapped up. "Your voice on the monitor woke him."

"Oops. Sorry. I forgot about that." And then she cringed. That meant Pierce had heard her singing silly songs and babbling nonsense to Cody.

She hid her hot cheeks by bending and lifting the crying child, who immediately tucked his face in her neck. She kissed the top of his head in the same noisy fashion she had Cody's. It made him smile through his tears just as she'd hoped. "Good morning, Graham."

Holding both boys, she shifted her attention to Pierce only to find his gaze raking over her not with disapproval of her casual attire but with heat, with hunger. Her pulse rioted and her mouth dried. How could he arouse her so easily and in the presence of the children?

"I—I don't know how Kat can stand to leave her baby. I couldn't bear to be away from Cody for days let alone weeks at a time. One of the reasons I loved teaching at the academy was because the on-site day care allowed me to visit him and hold him during my planning periods, but I've seen Kat's stories, and I understand the in-depth coverage can't be researched and written quickly. But how does she leave him?"

The words gushed from her like water through a broken dam, and she suspected she sounded like a ranting mad woman. But she had to say something, do something to distract Pierce before her knees buckled under his incendiary gaze.

His expression turned arctic, telling her she'd succeeded in dousing whatever flames had kindled. "Kat is an adrenaline junkie. Her goal is to take Christiane Amanpour's place. There was a time when I found her passion for her career quite attractive."

"You must have loved her very much." Did he still? Would he have people on the ground searching for her if he didn't? That had to be expensive.

"I didn't love her, and she didn't love me. Our relationship was convenient. Until she broke the rules. She never mentioned wanting a baby, and if she had I would have expected her to try to buy one on the black market, adopt from an underworld country or get inseminated at a sperm bank—anything that she could use as story material."

Anna gasped at his vehemence. "That's very harsh."

"Kat's career is her life, and ambition is her god. There's very little room for anything or anyone else."

How sad. If it was true. For him and for Graham.

"How do you do it?"

She blinked at his question. "Do what?"

"You treat Kat's son the same as your son even though he's only a temporary fixture in your life."

"With Graham or my students I try to make the moments I share with them some of their best memories. And yes, when my students move on a tiny piece of my heart goes with them. But I get my reward when children from previous years' classes greet me in the hall and give me bear hugs and huge smiles. Pierce, it's not all that difficult. All children really want is to feel loved and secure. That's all any of us want, isn't it?"

"Love doesn't guarantee happiness." Pierce shot to his feet. "I'll have my coffee in the kitchen."

Taken aback, Anna stared at his departing form. Getting him to bond with his son might be harder than she'd thought. His walls were high and fortified. But he'd touched Graham voluntarily, and that small step gave her hope.

Pierce had to get Anna out of his house, but to do that he had to get Kat home alive and well enough to take her son back to Atlanta.

He grabbed the phone and dialed his contact. "Find out who has Kat, and offer them a million dollars or as much as it takes to get them to let her go," he ordered as soon as the man answered.

"We're trying, sir. But no one's talking."

"Money loosens tongues. Make them talk." Pierce disconnected from his fruitless phone call, his frustration making him want to punch his hand through the glass pane of the French door in front of him.

Resisting Anna was getting harder with every moment she spent under his roof. He closed his eyes and pinched the bridge of his nose. He'd lain awake half the night thinking about his odd attraction to her.

He liked polished, career-focused, self-centered women. They didn't mind his dedication to Hollister Ltd. or the long hours he worked because they did the same. When they could carve out a block of time for sexual gratification they made sure they got what they needed then left. It was efficient, uncomplicated and satisfactory.

Anna was the complete opposite. She didn't fuss over

her appearance, but worse, she gave and expected nothing in return. Sex with her had been neither efficient nor uncomplicated.

And yet he wanted her.

It wouldn't be difficult to convince her to give him more of that sweet body, to allow him to do all the things to her, with her, that rolled though his mind when he should be sleeping. Those inappropriate thoughts had driven him from his bed to his office early this morning where he'd found her already in place. Working on his project.

He'd sent her upstairs to change because if he hadn't he wasn't convinced he'd have been able to keep his hands off her. Then she'd returned looking like an all-American girl with her jeans clinging to those long slender thighs and sent his already-primed libido into overdrive.

Holding her son had rucked up her shirt hem, revealing a strip of skin between her jeans and her top, and instantly an image of her breasts, the same pale cream shade and tipped with peachy nipples, had filled his head. He ached to taste, to touch, to explore every inch he'd missed last time.

Damn her. Damn her to hell for unleashing this beast he had never had trouble controlling before. Even now, he strained for a sound of her, indicating her whereabouts. Earlier she'd followed him to the kitchen to feed the slime crew breakfast. He'd grabbed his coffee and run.

Run. In his own home.

Anna Aronson was either the real deal or very, very good at laying her trap. He was beginning to suspect she was the former, which only reinforced his urgency to shed her and her son.

Before he took her back to his bed.

And then Anna breezed back into the office with sun-kissed cheeks and smelling of the outdoors, and he knew he was doomed to fail.

* * *

"The boys are down for their naps. I need more applications." Anna dropped her handful of pages into the rejection bin then turned to face her boss.

The passion in his eyes slammed the air from her lungs. When he looked at her as if she was the most desirable woman on the planet it was difficult to remember what she'd been about to say.

"How long will they sleep?" he asked, approaching with a measured tread that made her heart pound like a bass drum. His intention was as clear as a neon sign.

"Pierce, remember we decided this was not a good idea. We have work to do and we want…different things."

Or did they? Hadn't she told him this morning that all anyone wanted was to feel loved and secure? And if he could be taught to acknowledge those needs then maybe he wouldn't attempt to fill the void by submerging himself in his work to the exclusion of everything and everyone else.

"You want me." His deep, husky voice reverberated through her.

Lie. But she couldn't. "Yes, but—"

"And I want you. We can satisfy each other. While you're here. What could be simpler? As long as you don't try to make more of it than the brief affair it is."

It wasn't simple at all. Getting more deeply involved with him was very, very complicated. And risky. And she'd realized after their last encounter that casual sex wasn't for her.

But maybe she'd had first time jitters and that was why she'd felt something was missing. He made her feel good. Oh, so good. How could exploring that just a little bit more be wrong?

And hadn't she decided that remnants of the wounded child still resided somewhere inside this man's supremely sexy body? Maybe she could help heal him and teach him to trust again by using their overwhelming physical attraction.

"Okay."

"This has been driving me crazy." He touched her hip with a fingertip, then lightly scraped his nail across her abdomen just above her low-riding waistband.

Her stomach muscles contracted in surprise and delight. Goose bumps dotted her skin and she shivered, yet she wasn't cold. No, not at all. Heat coursed through her.

"Do you like that?"

"Yes. I like it when you touch me." Her cheeks warmed. She wasn't used to verbalizing her sexual needs.

"I can see you do." Using both hands he drew half-dollar size circles around her areolas, his consecutive rings growing smaller and smaller until he bumped over her puckered nipples. Another bolt of pleasure arced toward her center. Her lids fluttered closed.

He lingered, teasing the tips into hard little knots and making her ache deep inside. She squirmed, rubbing her knees together, trying to relieve the building tension.

He drew a path downward, flicked open the button of her jeans and lowered the zipper. She could barely hear the rasp over her pulse booming against her eardrums, but she could feel the giving way of each metal tooth quaking through her. Then his hand dipped inside, slipping beneath her panties and going unerringly to the source of her hunger.

He delved into her dampness and stroked upward, forcing a moan from her lungs. The noise sounded earthy and sensual and so unlike her. Her legs quivered as he repeated the caress again and again until she neared the edge. But she didn't want to do this alone.

She stilled his hand by pressing it to her. "I need to touch you too."

He withdrew his hand, only to grasp her shirt and tug it

over her head. He stared. "You have beautiful breasts. The skin is creamy and—"

"Freckled." She hated her pale, spotted skin.

"Like cinnamon sprinkles for me to taste." He bent and swept cool lips along the lace edge of her bra, and then his hot tongue followed. Oh my. She grabbed his waist to steady herself then fisted his shirt, eager to get rid of the barrier.

He lifted his head. "Impatient?"

"Yes."

He rewarded her honesty by ripping off the garment and tossing it aside. Then his attention returned to her.

She was caught up in admiring his broad chest when he snapped open the back hooks of her bra, skimmed it down her arms and then cupped her breasts. His warmth surrounded her while his thumbs brushed the tips, making her writhe in enjoyment.

"C-condoms." She couldn't believe she'd remembered.

"I have one. You—" He shook his head. "Let's just say I realized I'd better be prepared with you around." He pulled his wallet from his back pocket, extracted the packet and dropped both wallet and condom on the table beside the burgundy leather chair.

He meant to make love in here. In the study.

The realization heightened her response, making the fine hairs on her body rise and pushing her heart rate even higher.

He grasped her hips and pulled her close. The hard ridge of his erection pressed against her sent adrenaline pulsing in her veins. "Feel what you do to me."

She licked her lips. "You do that to me too."

And then he kissed her. Finally. His lips coaxed hers apart and then he devoured her mouth. She kissed him back, loving the wet, demanding carnality of the embrace. Her bare breasts nuzzled against him. She mapped his shoulders, his back, his narrow waist, relishing the supple skin stretched over hard muscles, and then she brazenly stroked his buttocks. He had a nice butt, not flat like so many men, but well-defined gluteus maximi. She smoothed her hands over the bunching muscles.

He released her and toed off his shoes, then unbuckled his belt. Thinking he expected her to do the same, she reached for her jeans.

"No. Let me." He stripped away the remainder of his clothing and stood before her blatantly aroused and with a confidence she envied.

Wanting to feel him, she reached forward then hesitated and met his gaze. "May I?"

His eyes widened as if her question had surprised him. "Of course. I want your hands, your mouth on me, Anna. And I want mine on you. Wanting to know how you taste has kept me up nights."

She gasped at his gravel-tone words then curled her fingers around his length. Searing. Satin. Smooth and hard. Like marble. Only hot. So hot. His breath whistled, and the tendons of his neck rose.

She did that to him. The knowledge emboldened her. She stroked him up, down, up again, savoring his raspy breaths and unfamiliar textures. Her thumb glided over his smooth swollen head, catching and spreading a drop of moisture.

With a deep chest groan he backed out of reach and sat in the wingback chair. "Come here."

Uncertain what he intended, she shuffled forward. He hooked his fingers in her belt loops and pulled her between his splayed legs, unclipped the baby monitor from her hip and set it on the table, then he pushed her jeans and panties over her hips and down her legs with the ease of a man who'd done it before. Often. Slightly daunted, she kicked off her sandals and stepped free of her pants.

His fingertips danced over the sensitive skin behind her knees, then glided up the backs of her thighs. His palms caressed her legs, first the outside, then he worked his way to the insides, nearing but not quite reaching her center. The slow methodical caresses were torture and heaven simultaneously.

He leaned forward and captured her breast with his mouth then proceeded to drive her into delirium with his lips, tongue and gently grazing teeth. Not wanting him to stop, she cradled his face and held him close. She traced his ears then dragged her short nails across his nape, his broad shoulders, down his spine. He shuddered and goose bumps lifted the skin of his back.

And then he sat back, leaving her damp nipples to cool in the office air. "I want to taste you."

She flushed hot all over. "I want to taste you too."

A lopsided smile lifted one corner of his mouth, and her heart turned over. "That might have to wait until next time."

Next time. The words hung on the air, heavy with promise.

He patted the arms of the chair and she frowned, not understanding his silent demand. "I don't...what...?"

"Put your knees here."

She bit her lip, hesitant, unsure. The curved chair arms were wide and padded, but still...

"Trust me, Anna, I won't let you fall."

Cautiously, she moved forward, planting her left knee on one armrest. He cupped her bottom and lifted, allowing her to place her right knee on the opposite side. Unsteady, she gasped and grabbed the back of the chair for balance and then looked down. Her precarious perch positioned her most personal parts right in front of Pierce's face. His mouth. Oh my.

His grip tightened, his fingers digging into her bottom. He pulled her forward, then his tongue flicked out to caress her most intimately, igniting her. Within seconds his skillful manipulations made her forget all about her unstable platform.

All she could do was feel each slick caress, the strength of his hands supporting her, the silk of his hair tickling her belly.

Tension built until pleasure pummeled through her, pounding her with wave after wave of ecstasy. She'd barely caught her breath before he did it again and again, each time leaving her weaker until her quaking muscles felt as if they'd disintegrated. She wasn't sure she could maintain her balance another second. "Pierce, I can't... I don't think... My legs—"

"Don't move." His order sounded more growl than man.

She looked when she heard cellophane tear and watched him hastily don protection, then his hands were back on her hips, supporting her weight.

"Straighten your legs. Don't worry. I've got you."

Warily, she extended one leg so that only the back of her knee was in contact with the chair, then the other. He lowered her, his arms quivering with the effort of supporting her full weight. The thick tip of his erection pressed her opening, and then he eased her down, down, down over him until he filled her completely. Her lungs emptied at the depth of his penetration. Never had she ever taken a man so deeply. And oh, it felt so, so good.

She opened her eyes and found herself staring directly into his. The intimacy of the position shocked her. They were face to face, breasts to chest, and the hunger burning in his eyes magnified hers exponentially. She shifted her hands from the chair back to his shoulders, feeling his muscles contract as he lifted her, lowered her, setting a rhythm that intensified the pressure building inside her.

Each time he seemed to go deeper when she knew that couldn't be possible since he'd already reached her soul. And then he arched his hips and met her descent and another orgasm shattered through her.

Somehow she kept her eyes open watching him watch her and it was more of a turn-on than she would have ever suspected. The color of his cheeks darkened as her body rhythmically contracted around his, and his breaths rasped, fast and choppy. He picked up the pace, lifting, thrusting, nostrils pinching white, face straining, neck tendons contracting until she climaxed once more.

He groaned and jerked forward, his face pressing against her breasts as he spasmed again and again beneath her. His hot breaths scorched her skin. Then his grip eased. She sank down on him feeling him pulse deep inside her. His palms glided from her buttocks to her waist, up her sweat-dampened back and down again. The sounds of their panting breaths filled the otherwise silent room. Her body felt boneless, hot and wet, as if she had melted all over him.

His head fell back against the chair and he slowly lifted his lids. She stared into his hazel eyes as reality returned.

Reality and the realization that she was falling in love with her boss.

Nine

He might never be able to move again.

Total satiation weighted every muscle in Pierce's body to the chair, a result of the most phenomenal sex of his life. And that was saying something since he'd never shied away from adventure.

Anna shifted in his lap and the slick slide of her body against his sent a fresh blast of fire though his groin. He inhaled a deep breath of the musk and honeysuckle scented air and forced his heavy lids open. The tension on Anna's face was his first clue that she wasn't enjoying the same level of nirvana.

She grimaced as she tried to extricate herself from her unusual roost. Awareness dawned that she couldn't be comfortable with her legs hyper-extended behind the chair. Not that she'd been complaining earlier. But earlier he'd been supporting the majority of her weight.

"Easy. Let me help. I'll hold you. Get your legs under you. Right here. Beside me." He caught her waist and lifted her slightly as she planted a knee in the chair beside him, her warm calf flanking his thigh, and then the other bracketed him. She rose and he slipped from her body. He instantly missed the hot clinch, which was odd because in the past he'd been the one who initiated the separation from his partner. Women always wanted to cuddle, but today he was the one wanting to linger, to savor the moist heat of her body fused to his. But he let her go.

She gingerly climbed from his lap and stood uncertainly in front of his chair, her hands clasped in front of her glistening red curls as if she'd developed a sudden case of shyness. Her gaze ricocheted off his, bouncing around the room. She snatched up her jeans and shielded herself.

He wasn't ready to surrender the view. "What's your hurry?"

"The boys. Work. A shower."

She wanted to wash away what they'd done. The tables had turned yet again. And he didn't like it. He rose and captured her chin, holding his words until she looked at him. The wariness in her light blue eyes surprised him.

"Regrets?"

Her lids fluttered closed. She sighed then opened them again. "No."

He searched her face and for once couldn't read her expression. There was more going on here than he could work out. What? No, best not to ask. He'd learned to avoid deep emotional conversations with women. His best bet was to focus on the facts. "I like how you taste."

Her cheeks turned crimson, dark enough to camouflage her freckles. She did that thigh swishing thing and his pulse jumped. "I—oh—thank you."

"And I like how you feel hot and wet surrounding me. Tonight after the boys go to bed—"

She abruptly backed out of his reach. "I really need to

get my shower and dress before they wake. I'll, uh…see you later."

She scooped up the rest of her clothes, providing a delicious but all too brief view of her derrière, then bolted naked from the room.

He wasn't exactly sure what had happened here besides mutual orgasms, but he was certain of one thing. It would happen again.

In love with Pierce Hollister.

Or maybe she was simply infatuated and she'd get over it.

Fat chance.

Anna kicked Cody's ball a little too hard. A stiff breeze caught it, carrying it into the air and off course. It splashed down in the pool. The resulting waves set off the pool alarm. The shrill noise rent the air.

Cody slapped his hands over his ears. Graham startled and his sweet face scrunched, indicating pending wails. She scooped up Graham and the quilt she'd spread on the grass.

"Oops. Sorry, boys. It's okay. The ball's taking a swim. Let's play out front."

She didn't dare try to retrieve the toy with her charges hot on her heels. One of them might topple into the water. The siren would turn off as soon as the waves settled. Almost as if she'd willed it the screech silenced.

"We'll race you to the front yard, Cody."

Cody squealed and took off running, his chubby little legs churning. She kept her pace slow enough for her son to remain two steps ahead. When she reached a shady area on the front lawn she set Graham down and laid out the quilt.

The boys wandered off to explore the new terrain while she mulled her problem. She loved that Pierce had established a scholarship for disadvantaged students and that he took time to personally read each application in its entirety even though it was often clear from the first page, sometimes even the first paragraph, that a candidate wasn't remotely qualified.

She loved that he'd hired a team to aid in securing Kat's safe release even though the woman had done him dirty with the most personal of betrayals.

She loved the way he watched Graham with a mixture of awe, fascination and fear. He could be taught to handle the fear. The former two gave her hope.

She'd had wounded children in her class before and eventually she'd won them over, but the process was never fast or easy. She'd have to convince Pierce he was worthy of love and get him to accept it. Then and only then would he be able to return the sentiment.

Helping him heal had become more than just a mission for Graham's sake. Now it was personal. She and Cody had a stake in the outcome.

A shrill sound interrupted Pierce's shower.

He shut off the water and tried to identify it. Smoke detector? No. The pool alarm. The floating device was set to go off if one of the boys fell into the water.

His heart rammed against his chest. He threw open the glass door, grabbed a towel and ran, haphazardly drying off as he streaked through the house. The eardrum piercing screech stopped as he thundered down the back stairs and into the kitchen, but he didn't slow down. His wet feet slipped on the tile floor.

He paused to secure the towel around his hips, yanked open the back door and scanning the yard, raced to the pool's edge. Cody's blue ball floated on the water's surface, but there was no sign of Anna or the boys in or around the pool area. And no child in trouble.

His panic subsided then reasoning kicked in. What had

set off the alarm? The ball? If so, the wind must have blown it into the water. But Anna was meticulous about picking up the toys and putting them away. She wouldn't have left it out here to get blown away.

Where were they? He could hardly walk down to the river's edge in a towel to search. He debated it for a half-second anyway, but then returned to the house. "Anna!"

Silence. He climbed the stairs. "Anna!" he called again even though he knew from experience that voices traveled through the house and she should have heard him the first time…unless she was giving the boys a bath. But she wasn't in the nursery or the bathroom. If the trio wasn't inside they had to be outside.

Sarah was still under the weather and the car was at her hotel. Pierce had insisted David keep it while he was in town caring for his wife. If Anna, Graham and Cody had gone somewhere they'd gone on foot.

He returned to his room and quickly dressed then jogged back downstairs, into the backyard and down to the boat dock. He searched the shoreline in each direction. No one walked the river's edge.

He tried to be comforted by the knowledge that Anna wouldn't let anything happen to the boys. He'd bet she'd guard her son with her life. And Graham's. He didn't know how she survived repeatedly getting attached then having those bonds severed.

He pivoted and studied the house. He hadn't heard the chime indicating the front gate opening, so if they hadn't left the property via the back they had to be in the walled yard somewhere. He retraced his steps but detoured around the side of the house.

In the front yard he spotted Cody chasing a butterfly with Graham toddling on his heels. Anna sat on a blanket in the grass watching them with her legs stretched out in front of her. The lilt of her laughter carried toward him on the breeze.

Relief flooded Pierce. He bent, parked his hands on his knees and paused to catch his breath and let his racing heart slow. Part of him wanted to yell because the pool alarm she'd insisted on installing had scared the living daylights out of him. But he reminded himself that meant the mechanism worked. If one of the boys had fallen in he might have reached him in time.

That might disturbed him. A heavy weight settled in his gut at the thought of either Graham or Cody getting hurt… or worse, and that was a far cry from his desire just days ago to get the trio the hell out of his house.

He straightened and found Anna looking directly at him. Worry lines marred her face. "Are you all right?"

"Yes." He wasn't about to tell her he felt as if he'd run a marathon—exhausted, winded, weak. He closed the distance and eased down onto the quilt beside her. "I heard the pool alarm."

She wrinkled her nose. "I'm sorry. The ball went in and I didn't dare try to retrieve it with this curious crew beside me. I'm trying to teach them that the stone patio surrounding the pool is off-limits. We play in the grass only."

She wore the clothes he'd peeled from her earlier and the scent of their lovemaking emanated from her. A fresh wave of arousal made his body sit up and take notice. How could he possibly want her again so soon? But he did. He wanted to lay her back on the blanket and strip her bare. Right here. Right now. But that wasn't going to happen with the dynamic duo around.

"No time for a shower?"

Her cheeks pinked. "No. Cody was already awake when I got upstairs. His singing woke Graham. You?"

"I heard the alarm about the time I lathered up."

Her lips curved in a sympathetic smile and her gaze slipped to his right ear. She lifted a hand, hesitated then lowered it again as if uncomfortable with touching him. She'd touched more than his ear earlier. "That explains the suds beneath your earlobe."

He reached for the spot and found slippery foam. "Guess I'm going back in." He noted her tangled auburn hair—hair he'd mussed when he'd kissed her—and recalled that first morning when he'd found her in the kitchen with bedhead and sleepy eyes. She hadn't even had time to brush her hair before the boys had demanded her attention.

"I never considered that you couldn't bathe when you wanted because of the boys."

She shrugged. "Learning to time your needs around the children's is part of being a parent."

Suddenly he felt like an abusive employer, and damn it, he prided himself on Hollister Ltd. being one of the most desirable places to work. "I'll get the housekeeper to give you more breaks."

"Pierce, you're the one who pointed out that I'm being well-compensated for my overtime. Don't worry about it."

He gave into the compulsion to smooth the tangled strands, savoring the glide of the thick satiny locks between his fingertips. He wanted to feel them brushing across his chest, his abdomen and lower—something the incendiary sex in the office hadn't allowed. He cupped her nape and tugged her forward.

"You look good with bedhead."

Her breath caught and she blushed. "The boys—"

He glanced at them investigating the in-ground sprinkler head. "They're fine."

And then he captured the "oh" of her soft lips and tasted the sweetness of her mouth. After a brief hesitation her tongue swept his and her palm pressed over his heart. His temperature and pulse rate skyrocketed. How did she evoke such an intense response so quickly?

He reminded himself that new affairs always burned hot. And then they burned out. This one would follow the same pattern.

A childish squeal startled him into lifting his head. The boys had discovered something—a toad by the looks of it. The amphibian hopped and Cody mimicked it. Graham tried and failed, but their antics made Pierce laugh.

"Go take your shower," he shocked himself by saying.

"But—"

"I'll watch them." He couldn't believe he was volunteering to supervise the children, but Anna deserved an uninterrupted shower. That didn't mean he was getting attached to the boys or her. He was simply trying to be a decent boss and a considerate lover.

Still, she hesitated.

"Go, Anna," he repeated before he wised up and changed his mind. "And take your time. I've got this."

He watched her leave with more than a little trepidation. The front door closed behind her. "Well, guys, it's just us."

Graham toddled over. "Da da da."

Pierce opened his mouth to negate the claim, but closed it. What was the point? The boy couldn't understand complex adult relationships.

Then Graham climbed into Pierce's lap. Pierce didn't have the heart to push him away. Instead he watched him play with his fingers, tug at his shoestrings, then the kid sighed, popped his thumb into his mouth and snuggled his warm little body into Pierce's chest the way Pierce had seen him do with Anna. Seconds later Graham turned into a dead weight.

Had the boy fallen asleep? One look at the dark lashes fanning flushed cheeks and Pierce had his answer. Adrenaline shot through his veins along with a strong urge to escape, but moving might wake the boy, and one scream-fest session was enough to last Pierce a lifetime. So he sat, the only things moving were his eyes as he supervised Cody.

Graham's little body started to tilt. Pierce lifted his arms, lowered them, then lifted them again to support the small child. His palm spanned the boy's entire back.

So little. So trusting. So much trouble. So not part of Pierce's life plan.

Cody joined them, his big blue eyes—Anna's eyes—taking in the scene. Pierce didn't have a clue how he'd hold two boys even though Anna made it look easy. He hoped Cody wouldn't ask.

"Gam seepin'."

"Uh yes, Graham's asleep."

"Odie not seep." The butterfly flitted past, catching the boy's attention.

Pierce said a silent thank-you as the carrot top followed the insect back to the shrubbery. Pierce looked down into the anchor in his lap and spotted a cowlick in Graham's dark hair. The same cowlick Pierce paid his stylist handsomely to disguise.

What would he do if Kat didn't make it home? Anna's question from days ago suddenly sprouted in his head. He didn't want to be responsible for Kat's child. But what else could he do? A knot rose in his throat as he weighed his options.

He couldn't send Graham into the system—not after the way child services had failed Sean.

Adoption? Graham was still young enough, cute enough to be adoptable. But the idea of strangers raising the boy, of never knowing if Graham was getting the care or attention he needed, made Pierce's stomach churn.

The only choice left was to keep him if Kat didn't come home. Pierce's heart pounded so hard it was a wonder it didn't wake the tot sleeping against him. If absolutely necessary, he'd take care of Graham the way Hank had Pierce with nannies and boarding school. It hadn't been an ideal childhood, but it beat the alternative.

The idea of shipping this kid off to a sterile dormlike environment didn't sit well. But it was the best he could do. He was not father material.

He hoped like hell that Kat made it home and he wouldn't be put to the test.

Despite Pierce's instructions to take her time, Anna rushed through her shower. She didn't want him thinking she was taking advantage of their new relationship to get out of doing her job.

She raced down the stairs and out the front door only to stop when she saw Pierce with his son asleep on his lap. Her heart melted a little.

The child couldn't be comfortable folded up like that, but the fact that Graham slept so heavily in his daddy's lap and more importantly, that Pierce allowed him to, was too valuable a moment to destroy.

Cody was still galloping after the butterfly, but when he saw her he ran over. "Up, Mama. Catch it."

"We can't catch it, sweetie. That would hurt the butterfly." She scooped him into her arms and kissed his brow, her gaze meeting Pierce's over her son's head.

The tenderness on Pierce's face quickly morphed into relief then a blazing inferno of desire as those hazel eyes swept down her body then up again. Her stomach felt as if she'd swallowed an entire flock of Cody's butterflies, but she forced herself to move forward on legs that quivered with reciprocal need.

"He has my cowlick," Pierce rumbled in a low voice.

"I told you he looked like you. He even has some of your mannerisms."

"That's impossible."

"Is it? Who's to say what's nature and what's nurture?"

"Down, Mama, down," Cody insisted and Anna set him back in the grass.

"Cody has bits of his father in him even though they've never met." She shrugged. "So who knows what's on our DNA?"

"Does it bother you to see your ex in him?"

"No. In fact, I hope Cody inherits some of his father's musical ability."

"Still love him? Todd, was it?"

"Any love I had for Todd died the day he willfully turned his back on his child."

Pierce's face tightened, and she realized he'd taken her words as a criticism. "You believe I did the same."

"I understand your reasons for rejecting Graham, but however he came into this world, he is a part of you. He is your son. Let me take him and put him in his bed where he'll be more comfortable."

"Are you sure you want to risk waking him? He's louder than the pool alarm when he's unhappy."

"He does have a healthy set of lungs, but his sleep schedule has been disturbed lately. It's best if we can get him back into a routine."

She squatted. Her fingers brushed Pierce's chest as she took Graham, and her body heated. Then she noticed the baby's flushed face and laid her fingers against his cheek. "He feels a little feverish."

Pierce stiffened. "What do we do?"

"Watch him for now. A little fever is a good thing. It helps fight the virus, but if his fever gets higher we'll need something to bring it down and we'll need to find a pediatrician. It would help if you knew the name of his doctor in Atlanta so we could get Graham's history."

"I don't."

"Don't worry. It probably won't be necessary. Let's go fix dinner, Cody."

She carried Graham inside. Pierce and Cody kept pace beside her, the former opening the door then heading for his office. Upstairs she laid Graham in his bed and once again touched his face. Sudden fevers weren't uncommon with children, but she'd need to watch him. She hung the monitor on the side of his crib.

"Odie eat."

"Yes, sweetie. It's almost time for dinner. I'll make a tent for you to play in while I'm cooking."

"Tent!"

His excitement made her grin. She grabbed a sheet from the linen closet and piggy-backed Cody downstairs. Pierce walked into the kitchen as she was draping the table, a stack of applications in his hand. She considered it progress that he wanted to work near them instead of locked away in his office.

"What are you doing?" he asked.

"Keeping Cody occupied while I prepare dinner."

An array of emotions chased across Pierce's face so quickly she couldn't make them out. "Sean and I used to play in a tent beneath the dining room table. I'd forgotten."

Her heartstrings twanged. "He was a lot older than you."

"Seven years. He was my hero." He pulled out a chair and sat. His eyes turned toward Cody, but his expression remained vacant. "He came looking for me after he left the system. He was eighteen and wanted to take care of me. Hank sent him away. I begged Hank to let me go with Sean, but Hank said I should consider Sean as dead to me as the rest of our family. And then he was."

Tears burned Anna's eyes. "Oh, Pierce. That was cruel. I'm so sorry."

"That was Hank. 'Forget the past. It's over,' he'd say. 'Live in the present and plan for the future.'"

"But if the memories are good ones why wouldn't you want to hold on to them?"

"Because you can't change the past. You can only shape your future. Reminiscing is a waste of time."

"Your past shaped you. Every experience you've had—good or bad—has brought you to where you are today. Denying or forgetting those events could make you disregard the lessons each taught you. I'm guessing your first eight years were pretty wonderful."

He exhaled. "They were."

She wanted to go to him so badly, to wrap her arms around him and comfort him. She settled for putting her hand on his shoulder and squeezing. "I know losing your mother, father and brother hurt, but they live on, Pierce. In you. And one day Graham's going to want to know how fantastic his grandparents were. He's going to want to hear stories about you and Sean. Don't deny him that."

His face shuttered.

She'd pushed hard enough. Anna left him to process their discussion while she got on with dinner. She was shredding cheddar for the macaroni and cheese when a strange sound came through the monitor. She paused. It almost sounded like Graham might be choking.

Dropping the grater and block of cheese, she turned off the boiling water and raced upstairs to his crib. Graham's face was contorted, his little body jerking. Her heart leaped to her throat. A seizure. She rolled him onto his side and made sure his airway was clear.

"What's wrong?" Pierce asked from behind her.

"He's seizing. Call the paramedics and open the front

gate." When he didn't immediately move she glanced over her shoulder. Pierce stood frozen, his face ashen with fear, his throat working. "Call them now, Pierce. We need help."

Ten

Pierce fisted his hands as he paced in the cramped space beside the emergency room bed.

He'd been useless, damn it, when Graham had needed him the most. If not for Anna's calm handling of the crisis— He broke off the thought, refusing to follow that path. He wanted Anna here now to promise him that the pale baby in the bed would be all right, but there had been room for only him in the ambulance with Graham.

Pierce stared at Graham who lay sedated, IVs in his arm and assorted other wires connected to his tiny body. How would he have told Kat if he'd let something happen to her child?

The curtain swished open and the doctor came in. "Does Graham have a history of seizures, Mr. Hollister?"

"I don't know."

"Does he have any allergies?"

When Anna had asked the same question weeks ago Pierce

had been irritated. Today panic swelled in his chest. He should know this stuff. "I don't know."

"You are his father, right?"

"Yes. Yes, I am his father," he admitted for the first time and with the acknowledgment came a huge weight of responsibility. Anna was right. Graham was his flesh and blood. His son.

The doctor looked at him strangely, expectantly. Pierce took a calming breath. "I am his father, but I don't usually have custody. Graham lives with his mother in Atlanta, but she is out of the country and can't be reached. She has never mentioned him having any health issues, and I can't get the information for you. I don't even know his pediatrician's name. But I am not allergic to anything, and I don't remember his mother being either if that helps."

"Good to know."

"When will he wake up?"

"Soon. We had to sedate him while we ran the MRIs and the EEG. That makes it easier on everyone—especially him. The good news is every test came back negative."

"Does that mean you'll stop treating me as if I hurt him?"

"I'm sorry. We do see cases of abuse, and we had to rule out an intentional injury. We often separate parent and child until we're certain. It's nothing personal."

It sure as hell had felt personal. "What caused Graham's seizure?"

"We're guessing it was a febrile seizure brought on by his rapidly rising temperature. Do you or your—his mother have a history of febrile seizures?"

"I don't know." He was beginning to hate those three words.

"Has anyone in the household been ill lately?"

"No—yes. My assistant. She came down with a high fever yesterday." Had it only been yesterday? It felt like weeks ago.

"Then it could be your son is coming down with the same virus."

"Will it happen again?"

"Probably, but if it's febrile seizures he's likely to outgrow them before he starts school. We'd like to keep him overnight just as a precaution."

Pierce stared at Graham lying so fragile and helpless in the big bed. A crushing sensation settled on his chest. The kid had slipped past his defenses. He'd let himself get attached, knowing full well that if—when—Kat returned home she'd take Graham back to Atlanta. For Pierce's own protection he'd have to reestablish the distance between him and the boy.

But not tonight. "I don't want to leave him."

"That's understandable, Mr. Hollister. The nurses on the pediatric floor will work with you. So if you'll step out for a few minutes and let us finish up here, we'll move your little fella upstairs to a room before he wakes." The intern held the curtain, a silent order for Pierce to leave.

Pierce couldn't move. He knew he needed to let the staff do their jobs to ensure Graham would recover, but—

A nurse touched his elbow. "Sir, we'll take good care of him. I promise."

Walking away from that bed, that baby, his son, was the hardest thing Pierce had ever done. Letting Graham, Anna and Cody go forever would be even harder. He was sure of it.

But he could do it. He'd survived worse.

And in the end, it would be the best course.

"Thank you for picking us up."

Even without the flat intonation of Pierce's voice, Anna could see his exhaustion weighting his shoulders and carving lines in his face. She'd felt it emanating from him during the silent ride home from the hospital.

"Why don't you take a shower and have a nap. No one sleeps well in the hospital. I'll take Graham."

She reached for the baby, but Pierce turned slightly away, his grip on the sleepy child tightening. "I'm fine."

She fell a little deeper in love with him at that moment. Yesterday he'd had a scare and he didn't want to let Graham out of his sight. Even though she hated to see Pierce suffering, his newly discovered attachment to his son proved he was becoming the loving father Anna had hoped he would be, and if he could love Graham, maybe he could find room in his heart for her and Cody.

"Mama," Cody squealed as he came galloping into the foyer with Sarah on his heels. Anna scooped him up, hugged him close and said a silent thank-you prayer for her son's good health.

Pierce's assistant had returned this morning, deeming herself eager to get to work even on Sunday to get the job done, then when Pierce had called just after lunch Sarah had volunteered to watch Cody while Anna went to collect father and son.

Pierce's tired gaze shifted to his assistant. "I'm happy to see you're feeling better."

"Thank you. Me too. I'm sorry my virus is likely what made your son sick. But you look like hell. Take Anna's advice and have a hot shower and rest. Anna and I have things under control."

"The applications—"

"Anna found your winner while you were at the hospital. She must have stayed up reading half the night. I've seen the submission and agree this is unquestionably the one. After you've rested I'll show it to you, but not before."

Anna bit her lip to keep from smiling at Sarah's bossy tone and waited to see if Pierce would put up with it.

"You are mothering me again."

"Someone needs to. Go. Put Graham in his crib on your way. Trust me, sleeping off this virus is the best way to get through it."

Pierce hesitated another few moments before climbing the stairs. Anna ached to go with him. Once he was out of sight Anna caught Sarah eyeing her speculatively. "Is something wrong?"

"I don't know what you've done to him. But I like it. I just hope he doesn't break your heart."

"My heart?" The organ in question fluttered wildly in her chest.

"You've fallen in love with him. I'll warn you, it won't be an easy road to travel, but my mother always said the folks that are the hardest to love are the ones who need it the most. That certainly applies to Pierce."

Anna opened her mouth to protest then closed it. She couldn't deny the truth. But Pierce had come a long way from the cold, isolated workaholic she'd first met. Maybe this would work out.

"Anna, why don't you follow him upstairs and see if he needs anything? I can see that you want to written all over your face."

Anna hoped she wasn't as transparent to her boss. "Cody—"

"Is fine with me. He's quite the little charmer."

"Yes, he is. Are you sure?"

"I'm almost back to my old self. Let's go make our snack, Cody."

"Odie hungee." Her son squirmed until Anna put him down then he lay his trusting hand in Sarah's and the duo headed for the kitchen.

Anna gathered her courage and climbed the stairs, hoping Pierce would accept her presence just as easily.

* * *

Pierce braced his arms on Graham's crib and tried to regroup. His life had been turned upside down since the little guy's arrival. But he was determined to set it right again and get back to his plan. Work would always be there. People offered no such guarantee.

He heard Anna approach even though she didn't speak. She stopped beside him, silently offering support. Her honeysuckle fragrance enfolded him, soothing his tattered nerves.

"How did you know what to do when Graham had the seizure?" he asked.

"I've had students with epilepsy before. I made it a point to learn how to care for them during an episode."

"I didn't have a clue."

"Most people don't. But febrile seizures usually only happen at the onset of an illness. Graham shouldn't have another one with this virus."

"And you know this how?"

"Internet." She smiled and something lightened inside him. He ought to push her away and begin the inevitable separation that would put them back on a boss/employee footing. But he didn't have the strength.

She placed a hand on his back, awakening his deadened senses. "I hear a hot shower calling your name."

An image of her body hot and wet against his made his heart pump harder, faster. "Join me."

"In the shower?"

Her shock-widened eyes made him realize that wouldn't be practical. "For my nap."

"I—we—Sarah—" She bit her lip and then nodded. "Okay. For a little while, then I need to relieve Sarah."

He had to smile at how easily she flustered. Catching her cool fingers in his, he led her to his bathroom, parked her on the vanity stool then disrobed. He liked the way her eyes followed every move, eating up every inch of skin he bared. Her pupils expanded, her cheeks peached and her lips parted, stirring him into full arousal even before he had removed his socks.

Her eyes widened when she caught sight of his reaction and her tongue slipped out to dampen her lips. He wanted her tongue on him so badly he almost said to hell with his shower. But he needed to wash away the hospital stench. And then he'd have her. Every luscious freckled inch of her.

Jumping into the stall, he lathered and rinsed in record time, conscious all the while of Anna watching, her fingers flexing as if she wished she were the one bathing his overheating skin.

The need to fill the void that had opened when he realized he had to let her go grew too urgent to ignore. He slapped off the water and dried quickly with the towel she handed him. He didn't bother with combing his hair. Instead he shoved it off his forehead with his fingers and reached for her.

She rose on tiptoe, meeting his mouth with soft lips. As good as she tasted it wasn't enough. He needed her naked against him. He made quick work of removing her clothing, dropping each item on the marble floor by their feet, then he set her away a few inches so he could admire her pale breasts with their puckered apricot tips. Looking wasn't enough. He tasted one, then the other, his hunger clawing impatiently in his gut.

He greedily mapped every curve of her smooth skin, palming, stroking, buffing, and when he caught the reflection of her back in the mirrors he briefly contemplated taking her here on the vanity counter where he could watch each thrust of his body into hers.

But no. Their last time together shouldn't be rushed. He wanted to go slow, to savor each second, each taste, each scent, each breath. He carried her to his bed and laid her on the sheets, wishing he had the time to count her freckles. But that would take all day and he didn't have the patience or luxury of time.

She extended her arms, inviting him into her embrace, but first he had to taste her sweet nectar one last time. He kissed her mouth, tangling tongues, and parted her lower lips with his fingers, finding her already wet, aroused and ready. That made two of them. But not yet.

He moved south, sampling the tips of her breasts and the heady fragrant skin beneath before moving on to her navel and the auburn triangle of curls. He found her swollen bud and flicked it with his tongue. She gasped and arched off the bed. He cupped her bottom and held her captive. Determined to make their last time their best, he ravaged her with his mouth.

He licked and sucked, driven by the music of her whimpers and moans, then when her body tensed telling him she was on the verge of climax he took her with his fingers, feeling the intimate clench and anticipating her taking him inside. She quaked and quivered, then her muscles contracted around him. But one orgasm wasn't enough. He wanted her to remember this. Remember him. He drove her over the edge again and again until she lay limp in his grasp.

"Pierce, please. I need you."

Her breathless voice broke his control. He climbed up her body and between the legs that had starred in more than a few of his dreams. He almost forgot the condom—a graphic illustration that he'd let her get too close. He yanked open the bedside drawer and impatiently took care of business.

He held her gaze as he sank inch-by-inch into her hot embrace. Desire smoldered at the base of his spine. His body urged him to fan the flames and race to the inferno, but he held back, trying to build slowly, trying to savor each squeeze of her body, each brush of her fingertips. Sweat dampened his skin at the effort.

Anna linked her ankles behind his back and lifted to meet each thrust. Her short nails scored his back, not hard enough to hurt but enough to shake his control, then she rasped across his nipples and the dam exploded.

He couldn't hold back his release another second. It broke over him in wave after wave of blistering heat, and when the spasms ended he was spent, more spent than he'd ever been in his life. He collapsed like a house of cards. Anna's hands stroked his back, soothing him, relaxing him.

When he found the strength he levered himself to his elbows, inhaling deep lungsful of sex-and-honeysuckle-scented air.

And he silently said goodbye.

It was time to rebuild the wall.

Déjà vu. Anna clutched the phone in her hand and knocked on Pierce's door. It had been an hour since he'd fallen asleep beside her, fifty minutes since she'd slipped from his bed and into her own room to shower.

Forty minutes since she'd checked on Graham and gone back downstairs certain Sarah would know exactly what Anna and Pierce had been doing in the master suite. But if his assistant suspected anything she hadn't mentioned it while they'd worked side-by-side writing the rejection letters.

Anna had been mulling over the difference in the way Pierce had lingered during this last round of lovemaking. Not that she was complaining about the excess of pleasure—far from it. But it had felt as if he'd been holding back. And then the phone had rung and from Sarah's set face, Anna suspected she wasn't going to like the outcome of this call.

Anna knocked again and when Pierce didn't answer she turned the knob. He was still in bed, still naked, lying facedown with the sheet covering his bottom half and a set of scratches down his back that only she could have given him. Her cheeks burned in embarrassment and in remembrance of how uninhibited he'd made her with that slow swiveling hip maneuver.

Blinking, he rolled to his side and scrubbed a hand across his face. "You're dressed."

"Yes. You have a phone call. Sarah said it's urgent."

He sat up, the sheet falling to his lap and revealing a mouthwatering display of masculine flesh. He extended his hand, forcing Anna to cross the room. The air smelled of him, of them and what they'd done. Her heart fluttered rapidly and desire weighted her midsection. Her body craved more of the same. Now.

He took the phone. "Hollister." His back went ramrod straight. "When?" He listened, closed his eyes, exhaled, his relief palpable. "Is she okay?"

Anna's nerves twisted tighter. The call could only mean one thing. And while she was happy for Graham, she wasn't sure where that left her and Pierce. When Kat returned Anna was out of a job.

He nodded. "Good. Fly her here. We'll be waiting." He disconnected and dropped the handset in his lap.

"Kat's coming home." He confirmed her thoughts.

"How soon will she arrive?"

"By morning. She's getting ready to board the plane now. I'll be down in ten minutes."

The last sounded suspiciously like a dismissal and his face…his face looked as tight and shuttered as it had the day she'd met him. Why did this feel like the beginning of the end?

Pierce opened the front door and a tall blonde flung herself at him and clung to him as if she'd never let go. His hands rested on her waist, not embracing, but also not pushing away.

Anna couldn't see his face to read his emotions. Her insecurities gathered like a flash mob, crowding in from every direction all at once. Pierce and Kat shared a history and their son ensured they'd share a future. Did he still have feelings for the mother of his son?

Kat finally stepped back. She looked a lot thinner and paler than the woman Anna had seen on TV, but that didn't diminish her beauty. "Thank you for whatever you did to get me out of there."

"You're welcome."

"Daddy will repay—"

"Forget it."

"Where's Graham?" Kat scanned the foyer and her intensely green eyes landed on Anna and Graham. Anna started forward. Kat rushed to meet her halfway. Graham launched for his mommy and Anna surrendered him along with a little piece of her heart.

Kat buried her face in his neck and held him as close as physically possible. To give her full credit, the shuddery breaths and the tears streaming down her face when she lifted it to look at her baby appeared genuine. "You have grown so much, peanut."

Anger blossomed inside Anna. She wanted to chastise Kat for going away without arranging more reliable child care for her precious son than a sitter who'd dump Graham on child services. But she held her tongue. Now was not the time. Let the woman have a peaceful reunion with her baby. Maybe Kat's experience had been a wake up call to what she stood to lose if she kept going into politically unstable countries.

Anna met Pierce's gaze over Kat's shoulder, but his blank expression gave no hint to his emotions. "Kat, this is Anna, the nanny who's been taking care of Graham."

The nanny. No mention of their intimate relationship. But

that would be awkward—almost as awkward as Anna lying in her bed last night and wondering if he'd come to her.

Anna forced a smile. "Graham is a sweetheart."

"Yes, yes, he is. And thank you."

"Your son has had a rough time since you took off," Pierce said. "Come into the study and I'll fill you in."

The trio left and a lump rose in Anna's throat.

Now the only question left to answer was where did that leave Anna and Pierce?

Eleven

Pierce watched the gates silently close behind the car carrying Kat and her son to the airport. A restless and uneasy feeling came over him.

Relief. That's all it was. He was no longer responsible for Graham. The past forty-eight hours had certainly proven he was not father material.

If not for Anna Graham could have ended up like Mike.

Anna. Another loose end. As soon as he dealt with her his life would return to normal, and he and Sarah could fly back to Arizona only two days behind schedule.

Mulling over his response to seeing Kat again—or more accurately, his lack of response—he closed the front door. He'd felt no desire for his former lover, but then things had been cooling down with them months before she'd betrayed him. Why else would he not have noticed her absence during the passing months before he'd discovered she'd betrayed him?

Their irregular hookups had been acceptable. He'd never

lost sleep when she cancelled one of their scheduled meetings at the last minute to chase a story lead. Nor had he counted the moments until her return—until he'd ended up with her child.

She'd been a miscalculation. He'd chosen her because she'd been as wrapped up in her career as he had been in his, and he'd been certain she would never demand more from him than he was willing to give—good sex and good times. He certainly would not have expected her to let a child interfere with her career.

But she hadn't, had she? She dumped Graham on a less than trustworthy child care provider and chased her ego-fulfilling career.

Anger burned in his chest. If it happened again—

What?

Nothing. Hadn't he already determined he didn't want to be a father and that the boy was better off with his mother?

Pierce dusted his hands mentally and physically. It was time to get his life back on track and his focus back on Hollister Ltd. But first, Anna.

All he had to do was cut her a check and arrange to have her and Cody driven to their apartment. Simple enough. So why was he lingering in the foyer instead of getting the job done? He had never been a procrastinator and he wasn't going to pick up the bad habit now.

"Anna." Pierce's voice carried up the stairs and into the nursery fifteen minutes after Anna had heard a car pull out of the driveway.

Her heart skipped a beat. She put down the book she'd been trying but failing to read and glanced at Cody, checking to make sure Pierce's call hadn't woken him, then she wiped her palms on her denim skirt and heeded the summons.

Pierce stood in the foyer at the bottom of the stairs. "My office."

He spun around and stalked off, leaving Anna to follow. She tried to ignore the trepidation settling over her and descended the stairs. Did he miss Graham already? Did he miss Kat? Was he emotionally withdrawing to handle the loss?

Where did this new state of affairs leave them?

He no longer needed a nanny and his vacation time was up. He'd be returning to his real world in…where? She realized they'd never discussed his work. Would he want her and Cody to come along or did he live close enough to visit? It wasn't as if she expected a commitment from him right away or anything. They needed time to get to know each other.

Marriage? The word shook her like an earthquake. Was she actually contemplating remarrying? She'd convinced herself after Todd that she never wanted to be subject to a husband's whims again. But she wanted to be connected to Pierce. She wanted him to know she would always be there for him. She wanted to love him and teach him to love back.

The discovery made entering his office all the more nerve-racking. Pierce sat behind his desk, wearing almost exactly the same forbidding expression as he had the day they'd met. She saw no trace in his eyes of the passion they'd shared this time yesterday.

Sarah rose. "I'm going to make a pot of coffee." The sympathetic look she aimed at Anna before leaving the room and closing the door added to Anna's disquiet.

"Kat and Graham are gone?"

"Her father is eagerly awaiting their return to Atlanta." He had a folder in front of him, which he offered to her.

With apprehension buzzing inside her like a hornet's nest she approached the desk and took the manila file without opening it. "When will you get to see Graham again?"

"I won't."

"But—"

"There is no 'but,' Anna. Nothing has changed. I am not Graham's father in any way other than biologically. He's better off with his mother."

Aghast, she stared at him. "How can you say that after you've spent time with him?"

"Easily. I have no room in my life for a child. If you'll look in the folder you'll see I've given you three months' severance pay in addition to a favorable recommendation letter."

Money. When what she really wanted from him was free. "That's too much. I only worked for you for two weeks."

"You earned it by working around the clock. I didn't realize what that entailed when I drafted the employment contract. Thank you for taking care of Graham. The car I've hired to take you and Cody home should be here within the hour." He stood, rounded the desk and opened the door.

Shock knocked the breath from her. "That's it? Thank you and goodbye."

"Yes."

"What about us?"

"I told you our association would last only as long as this job."

"Yes but—" She bit her tongue, trying to hold on to her pride even though her heart was breaking. She'd thought the temporary nature of their liaison had changed when he'd made love to her so beautifully. But he was dismissing her as he would any other employee and paying her for "services rendered." It made her feel cheap.

Pain crushed her chest and burned her eyes, but she would not cry. Not in front of him. Devastated, she realized that she'd been fooling herself once again—the same way she had when she'd believed if she'd been smart enough her father would love her and when she'd believed Todd's flattery meant he loved her and wanted more from her than just a meal ticket. Clearly, she could not trust her judgment.

Pierce was not going to change. The way he'd let his son walk out of his life was proof that he would never let down his guard and allow her and Cody into his life. He'd never love her the way she yearned to be loved.

She and Cody deserved someone who could love them despite the fear of losing them.

"I'll pack as quickly as I can." Gathering the tattered remains of her heart and her pride, she left the office and the man she loved behind.

"Ohmigod, ohmigod, ohmigod! I can't believe I won!" the young woman bounced up and down then grabbed her two-year-old's hands and danced in a circle with the little girl in the living room of her sparsely furnished apartment.

Her behavior and the child's resultant infectious giggles reminded Pierce of Cody, Graham and Anna. He rubbed his chest, battling a sudden acute case of heartburn.

"Congratulations, Nikki. You were the best candidate out of over a thousand applications."

Anna had chosen well. This young lady wasn't Hollister Ltd.'s typical scholarship recipient. Pierce readily admitted he would have discarded her application as soon as he'd read Nikki had become pregnant at fifteen. But Anna had seen potential.

Nikki had stayed in school and maintained a 4.0 grade point average. She'd graduated salutatorian from high school last year despite parenthood and a part-time job, and she was currently working a minimum wage job, taking one college class per semester and traveling to local schools to talk to young women about avoiding teenage pregnancy.

She wanted to be a teacher. Like Anna.

When Nikki finally stopped whirling, tears streamed down her face—happy tears, not the kind that made Pierce want to run. "You have no idea how much this means. I'll be able to set a better example for Leila, and once I graduate and get a real job, I'll be able to move her and Momma away from here."

She scooped up her daughter and hugged the little girl close. Her obvious love for her child again reminded him of a certain redhead.

He offered Nikki the engraved invitation. "The awards banquet will be on the twenty-seventh. Hollister Ltd. will fly you and your guests in for the presentation."

Nikki's smile wobbled then vanished as she studied the embossed words. "The banquet's on a Saturday? And all the way in Arizona? I can't go."

Her refusal left him momentarily speechless and in an unusual position. He looked at Sarah, who shrugged, then he turned back to Nikki.

"We've never had a recipient refuse to attend the awards celebration. Keep in mind that we'll be flying you and any family members you choose to Arizona on a private jet, and we'll put you up in a first class hotel. At our expense."

"That all sounds wonderful, Mr. Hollister, like a dream come true for a South Carolina Low Country girl like me. I've never been on an airplane or anywhere west of Greenville, but my mother is afraid to fly. Even if she wasn't, I work weekends. My boss can't handle the diner by herself. And I don't have anyone I trust except my momma to watch Leila for a whole weekend. So as amazing as this opportunity is, if I have to be there in person to accept, then I m-might ha-have to p-pass."

Uncomfortable with the woman's emotional struggle, Pierce looked away. He wanted to say, "She's not your mother. She's paid to take care of you." But he didn't. He studied the rundown apartment in the low rent district. It was clean, but it was obvious Nikki's foster family did without luxuries. This young lady was willing to sacrifice her future for her daughter's safety and the happiness of a family that wasn't related to her by blood.

Like Anna.

Damn it, everything reminded him of Anna these days. He pushed away the image of her smiling freckled face, not without difficulty. "What will your boss do once you're a full-time university student?"

"Oh, I plan to go to the local college. I promised her I'd still work weekends. I owe her too much to leave her in the lurch. She gave my momma a job when my foster dad left and me one as soon as I turned sixteen. Applying for your scholarship was actually her idea. She's like my honorary grandmother."

Nikki had made room in her heart for those who weren't related to her. Like An— He severed the thought. "Then I guess we'll have to bring the awards ceremony to you."

Sarah gasped and her eyes goggled. "Pierce—"

"We'll make the arrangements and get back to you."

And perhaps the chaos of relocating the awards banquet with only eighteen days' notice would keep him from thinking about Anna.

He and Sarah left the apartment and climbed into the waiting hired car. Once they were buckled in, Sarah turned to him. "You know there's a simple fix for what ails you."

"What are you talking about?"

"Call her. Call Anna. I think she'd like to meet Nikki."

"Anna has done her part. And you are mistaken if you think I'm 'ailing' for her."

"You have been a grouch these past two weeks and you pace your office like a caged lion. You have bags under your eyes that tell me you're not sleeping and you're losing weight. I think half the managerial staff wants to punch you. I'm in line right behind them. And you stare at every child we encounter like you're searching for Graham or Cody. You miss them. Admit it."

Sarah read him too well. He had his life back, his peace, his routine. Everything he wanted. But something was lacking from his predictable organized schedule. "I miss them. But I don't have room for them in my life. Not right now."

"I have news for you, Pierce. Life is not convenient. It's messy and complicated and requires compromise. Do you think it was convenient for Nikki to get pregnant when she was just a child herself? Do you think it was convenient for her mother to stand by her when Nikki's father told her to get rid of the brat or get out of his house? Do you think it was convenient for Anna to come home from the hospital with an infant and discover her dreamer of a husband preferred to be the only baby in their relationship?"

He straightened. "Anna told you that?"

"Of course not. Anna isn't one to speak ill of anyone, but what I gathered from our conversations is that her husband wanted one hundred percent of her attention and when he realized he wasn't going to get it, he left."

"Bastard. She is better off without him. And Anna, Cody and Graham are better off without me too. I know nothing about children, and my ignorance could end up getting one of them hurt."

"It's not only them getting hurt that scares you. You're afraid of loving them and losing them like you have everyone else. There are no guarantees of happy endings, Pierce. The only guarantee is that if you don't allow Anna and the boys to be a part of your life, you will lose them—if you haven't already."

Her words settled over him like a dense, chilling fog. "They would dilute my focus. Hollister—"

Her disgusted snort cut him off. "In all the years I've known you, you've never backed down from a challenge. You didn't tuck your tail and run seven years ago when Hank's board member buddies swore your inexperience would run the company into the ground and tried to force you to resign as CEO. Instead you decided to prove them wrong and came up with a plan to make them eat their words by doubling the company before Hollister Ltd. celebrated its fiftieth anniversary.

"I thought you were crazy. But you are on the verge of accomplishing that impossible task. What makes you think you can't do more? Do you want to die old and alone like Hank? Or do you want to fill your days—however many you have left—with people you love?"

"Hank wasn't alone. He had me."

"He kept you at a distance and treated you more like an employee than a son. The real winner in life is not the one who dies the richest, but the one who lives the richest, the one who sees value in not just gold bullion, but also in the simple things like oatmeal cookies, a child's laughter, holding a loved one's hand.

"Call Anna, Pierce. Invite her to the banquet—whenever you figure out when and where you're going to host it. And maybe she can help you see the light before it's too late. Because I am ready to wash my hands of you."

Determined to hide her frustration from Elle, Anna pasted a smile on her face and let herself into the apartment.

Elle looked up from the floor where she was playing trucks with Cody. Every time Anna saw the big yellow Tonka toy dump truck she was reminded of Pierce and her heart ached anew. The truck, along with a massive box of food and a new window herb garden, had been delivered the day after Pierce had dismissed her. She'd found a note inside the box that read, "To replace what you gave away."

Nothing personal or tender for her, but he'd sent a toy for Cody. And the gift had gotten her hopes up. For twenty days she'd jumped every time the phone rang or someone knocked on her door. But she'd heard nothing else from Pierce.

"Any luck finding that teacher?" Elle asked.

Leave it to Elle to get right to the point. "No. It's as if she's gone into hiding. None of my former coworkers has seen her since she quit the academy."

It had been three weeks since Anna had left Pierce's home, and she hadn't found a job. One good nanny reference wasn't going to be enough to overcome getting fired as a teacher. She had to clear her name, and that meant finding the teacher she'd replaced at the academy, a woman who'd apparently gone into hiding.

"Mr. Hollister called."

Anna's heart stalled. "What did he say?"

"He was just checking to see if you and Cody were okay, but he didn't leave a number and he said that you didn't need to call back."

"Anything else?"

"Nope. Not really. We just chatted about school and Cody and stuff, and then he had to go."

Anna's hopes sank. She had to quit believing in miracles. Pierce wasn't suddenly going to decide he couldn't live without her and Cody.

"Oh and I picked up your mail."

Anna followed Elle's nod toward the kitchen table. A heavy vanilla colored envelope sat atop the pile of junk mail like a flower in the desert. Anna crossed the room and picked it up. The engraved address on the back flap read, "Hollister Ltd. Bisbee, Arizona."

Arizona? Pierce was on the opposite side of the country? What could this be? The only thing she'd ever received on stationery of this quality was a wedding invitation. Was he marrying Kat?

Anna's skin turned clammy and cold. Feeling slightly sick

to her stomach, she carefully opened the flap and pulled out the heavy card inside. Hollister Ltd. cordially invited her to the Sean Rivers Memorial Scholarship awards banquet where Nikki Smith would be honored.

Nikki. So Pierce had stuck with Anna's choice. For some reason that pleased her.

She read the rest, shaking her head, because no matter how much she might want to see Pierce again, she could not afford to travel to the banquet's Charleston, South Carolina, location.

With a heavy heart she extracted the self-addressed, stamped reply card. Her hand shook as she checked the regrets box.

It was time to move on with her life and forget Pierce Hollister and the magic they'd made.

Pierce tossed Anna's RSVP onto his desk.

He wanted to call her and tell her she could not refuse. She'd chosen this candidate and she needed to see it through.

He wanted to see her. And Cody.

And Graham.

He'd spent too much time thinking about each of them since he sent them away, but especially about Anna. Her laugh. Her smiles. Her generosity. Her ability to open her heart even when the end was in sight.

The freckles he'd never had a chance to count.

Shaking his head, he reached for Hollister Ltd.'s most recent financial statement. The numbers should have filled him with satisfaction. He was on target to meet his goal. Instead, the emptiness remained. He'd been blaming the deep ache in his chest on heartburn. Now he knew better.

He'd fallen in love with Anna Aronson.

The financial statement fell from his hand. Love. He'd sworn to never let it happen to him. And now it had. What in the hell was he going to do about it? Pushing Anna away wasn't working. She inhabited his sleeping and waking hours.

He reached for the report his conversation with Elle had instigated. Elle had told him that Anna couldn't get a job until she cleared her name and that Anna had spent weeks searching for the teacher she replaced because she suspected the woman had experienced similar issues with the student's father as Anna had.

The teacher had been nearly impossible to locate, but Pierce only employed the best, and his man had tracked down the woman. She'd gone into hiding when she'd discovered she was pregnant by the father of one of her students. The father had been an influential donor at the school, she'd told Pierce's investigator, and he had tried to force her into an abortion. Her only option if she wanted to keep her baby had been to run.

Anna hadn't lied.

But then Pierce had known that deep in his gut for quite a while. Anna's honesty wasn't the problem. His cowardice was. Playing it safe and trying to stay unattached hadn't worked. Even though he'd tried not to care, didn't want to care, he did. While his head said to give himself more time to get over missing them, his heart knew it was too late.

Cutting Anna and the boys from his life had left a wound that wasn't going to heal. Just as the pain of losing his parents and Sean had never healed.

Pinching the bridge of his nose, he sat back. He had to make this right. And to do that he had to overcome his fear of loving and being left behind.

The task seemed Herculean. He didn't know where to start.

Anna would tell him to start with Graham. His son. Raising the boy as Hank had Pierce wouldn't work. He didn't want his son to be a stranger the way Pierce had been with Hank. He and his father had shared nothing in common except Hollister Ltd. And he didn't want to take Graham away from his mother. Kat might have her priorities screwed up, but she loved the boy.

Kat traveled a lot. Perhaps he could convince her to allow Pierce to keep Graham whenever she went out of town—several weeks every month. It wasn't much, but it was a start. He wanted his son in his life, and once he had those details worked out he'd go after Anna and Cody.

Because being alone was no longer good enough.

Twelve

The knock on the door Saturday morning startled Anna into dropping the spatula. Her heart quickened. She instantly chastised herself. It wouldn't be Pierce. It was probably Elle and Cody returning early from next door. But baking oatmeal cookies made her think of the man who'd broken her heart.

She opened the door to Pierce. Pierce. Her breath caught and her knees went weak as she drank in every inch of him from his intentionally messy dark hair to his hazel eyes and tightly smiling mouth. She visually devoured the black suit encasing his lean, muscular body, his white shirt and crimson tie and then settled on the big flat box tucked beneath one arm.

No. She wasn't over him. So much for five weeks of trying to forget him.

"Hello, Anna."

His voice warmed her like a sunbeam breaking through the clouds. "Wh-what are you doing here?"

"The scholarship banquet is tonight. You should be there since Nikki was your choice."

She sighed, battling disappointment. What had she expected? For him to say he missed her and loved her and couldn't live without her? Wasn't going to happen. Not with an emotionally unavailable man like him.

"I sent my regrets."

"And I refuse to accept them."

"It's in South Carolina, Pierce. Even if I wanted to go, I couldn't afford to and I wouldn't leave Cody."

"That's why I'm flying you and Cody and Elle to Charleston."

"Elle? Does that scamp know about this?" Was that why the teen had been smiling so much the past few days?

"Yes. But I asked her to let me surprise you, so don't chastise her."

His offer was tempting, but no. Quitting him cold turkey was the best way to get over him. "Pierce, me going away with you overnight is not a good idea."

"May I come in? Or must we discuss this in the hall for your neighbors' entertainment?"

"My neighbors look out for me." But she opened the door and stepped back. He crossed the threshold, immediately making her small den feel even smaller.

"Do I smell oatmeal cookies?"

"Yes." She rudely didn't offer him one.

"Elle will be your chaperone—if you need one. I bought a dress for you to wear tonight. Elle said purple was your favorite color."

Somebody was going to get a serious scolding.

"Try it on." He offered the box. She ignored it.

"Pierce—"

"I want you to meet Nikki and see how right you were about her. She's a remarkable young woman with a lot of potential. In fact, she reminds me of you—always putting others first."

His compliment sent another ray of light her way. She shook her head. "I'm happy that you approve of my choice, but I can't go."

"Elle's never been on an airplane or stayed in a hotel before. I've reserved a suite of rooms for the three of you. Elle's excited. Don't disappoint her."

Not fair! "You fight dirty."

"I like to win. Come on, I'll even help you with the zipper."

She could feel her resistance crumbling. "I'm sure you're better at getting women out of their clothes than into them."

"I'm multitalented. I can do both. Let me show you." He punctuated the sentence with a wicked grin that incinerated her good intentions.

She sighed. "Give me the dress."

He handed her the box. She took it without grace and backed toward her bedroom. He took a step forward. She pointed her finger. "You wait here."

She retreated, locking the door behind her—not because she didn't trust him, but because she didn't trust herself if he came through that door.

Curiosity took over. She lifted the lid, revealing a dress made of a deep purple stretchy fabric. She held it against her body. It didn't look like much—just a bunch of gathers and drapes.

She dropped it on the bed and shed her jeans and top then slid the dress over her head. It felt silky smooth sliding against her skin. She moved to the mirror above her dresser and blinked in surprise. Wow. The sleeveless design left her freckled arms bare, but no one was going to be looking at her arms.

The dress was a masterpiece of engineering and whoever had designed it was a genius. The gown turned Anna's average figure into an amazing hourglass shape. The fabric draped from her shoulders to form a subtly sexy V between her breasts. Not too much cleavage, but enough to get attention. An empire waist accentuated her curves and waist, then the fabric gathered just below her left breast to sweep at an angle over her lower half all the way to the floor.

The overall effect was elegant, sexy and impressive, if she did say so herself. She looked like a Grecian statue only better, and the color made her hair and skin glow.

A knock on the door made her jump. "You okay in there?"

Pierce. She wanted him to see her like this. Then maybe he would— No, she shook her head. He wasn't going to love her because of a dress. She shuffled to her closet, slipped on silver sandals then opened the door.

His eyes widened. His lips parted. His chest rose. Then his gaze slowly roved from her head to her toes and back again, his pupils dilating. "You look incredible."

The husky timber of his voice reinforced his comment.

"Thank you. The dress is amazing."

"It only accentuates the woman wearing it." His hazel eyes met and held hers. The chemistry was still there. She ached to throw herself in his arms, or better yet, drag him the few steps to her bed. But she wouldn't because she was smarter than that. Making love with him again would only make his inevitable departure hurt that much more.

"And there is no zipper. But good try."

He smiled. "A man's gotta do what a man's gotta do. Come to the banquet with me, Anna. Please."

When he put it like that how could she refuse? "Okay."

"I have something else for you." He reached into his inside coat pocket and extracted a business size envelope.

"What is it?" she asked even as she opened it.

"A notarized letter from the teacher you replaced stating that she succumbed to the advances of the same parent who came on to you. She had his older son in her class, and she says that when she became pregnant as a result of the affair with Dan what'shisname he ordered her to have an abortion. When she refused, he threatened to get her fired. Instead, she quit her job and went into hiding."

Flabbergasted she gaped at him. "How did you know I was searching for her? And how did you find her?"

"When I talked to Elle a couple of weeks ago, she said the dismissal was keeping you from getting a job, then she told me you'd been searching for your predecessor hoping that if you found her she could help you clear your name. And I found her because I only hire the best."

She supposed she should take that as a compliment.

"If you approve, on Monday my attorney will take a copy of this letter to the academy and demand the school give you a good reference or he'll take legal action. We can even force them to reinstate you or sue them for wrongful dismissal, if you wish."

"I don't want to go back there, not after the way the headmaster treated me. But what about this teacher? Couldn't she just call the headmaster?"

"She's asked that I keep her location secret. She chose to have and raise the child, and she'd prefer the father not be able to find her and possibly sue for custody. Like you, she'd rather have nothing to do with a man who could reject their child."

She pressed the letter to her chest. Vindication. Her reputation would be cleared. "Thank you."

"With your resume and credentials, you should be able to find another position. But I have a better idea." He shifted on his feet, looking uncharacteristically uneasy. "Marry me instead."

Shock stole her breath. "What?"

"I want you—and Cody—back in my life. Permanently."

She searched the face she'd come to love and she was

desperately tempted to say yes. But she couldn't. "Pierce, I won't settle for anything less than a man who loves unconditionally. You cut us—and your son—out of your life without a qualm."

He frowned. "A mistake. I honestly believed that if I tried hard enough I could keep myself from caring for you and the boys. But I was wrong."

He took her hands in his and for a moment she lost herself in the warmth and strength of his grip.

"I've fallen in love with you, Anna. With your smile, your laugh, your freckles, but mostly with the way you open your heart to anyone who needs it. I need it. I need you. My house is empty without you. I am empty without you. And work… just can't fill the void you left behind."

The words were perfect and her heart melted a little. But Todd had taught her that she needed more than pretty, meaningless words. She needed someone whose actions proved he meant what he said. "I'm not sure I can believe you."

"I've asked Kat for joint custody of Graham and she's agreed. I want to be a part of his life, to watch him grow up."

Her hopes deflated like an untied balloon. "Is that why you want me? To make taking care of him easier?"

He looked genuinely shocked by her words. "No. Yes. Both, I guess. But I am not looking for child care from you. I've been an emotional coward. But you…you love without fear. I want you to teach me how to do that. I want us to be a family again—the one you created. My life is richer with you and the boys in it."

Her heart filled with hope. She wanted so badly to believe him. But she needed proof. "I don't know, Pierce. This all seems very…convenient."

"Do you love me?"

She wanted to lie so badly. "That is not a fair question, and I—"

"Do you, Anna?"

She mashed her lips together, fighting the urge to yield the answer his eyes asked her to give, but something in his steady, compelling gaze made her will crumple. "Yes. But this isn't just about me. I have to think of Cody. I'm not sure you can be the father he needs."

To give Pierce credit, he took her rejection stoically. "Come to the ball tonight. After that…I'll work on proving to you that I can be the husband you deserve and a good father to our boys."

Our boys. Funny how two little words could glow with so much promise. They lit a spark of optimism in her skeptical soul. Maybe, maybe Pierce could back up his pretty words with action. But only time would tell.

"Congratulations," Anna said to Nikki at the conclusion of the awards banquet. Seeing this young woman's exuberant face seemed a fitting conclusion to Anna's whirlwind day of new adventures, including a flight on a private jet, a limo ride to a stupendously luxurious hotel suite and finally, attending a sumptuous banquet attired in her incredible evening gown.

Nikki beamed. "Thank you. And thank you both for giving me a chance. I'll prove that it wasn't a mistake."

Her words came a split second before Pierce's hand settled on Anna's waist. She knew it was him without looking because of the way her body reacted. Each tired cell in her body went on alert. "You're welcome."

Nikki waggled her fingers in farewell then rejoined her foster mother and followed the last of the guests from the banquet hall.

Anna suddenly felt nervous. Now that the festivities were over did Pierce expect her to sleep with him? She had to admit she was tempted despite her earlier vow to take it slow and keep this weekend platonic. He had been so attentive tonight, treating her like a princess. Every touch and glance had made her pulse pound. Her resistance was low.

She gave in to the compulsion to look into his eyes. The banked heat she saw in his face made her pulse skip. "It was nice of you to pay Elle to babysit Cody and Nikki's little girl."

"It was worth it to get you here."

"Pierce," a female said from behind them, and a chill dashed down Anna's spine. She'd recognize that voice anywhere. Kat.

She forced herself to turn and instantly wished she hadn't. Even in her glamorous purple gown, Anna would never be able to compete with Katherine Hersh in a basic black sheath. Apparently she'd attended the dinner. Anna was glad she hadn't noticed.

"Could I talk to you?" Kat said.

Only then did Anna notice the other woman's eyes were slightly red as if she had been crying.

"I'll go check on Elle." Anna tried to back out of Pierce's hold, but he caught her hand.

"No. Anything Kat needs to say to me she can say in front of you. You are a part of my life now. My business is your business. Let's go."

He led them through the hotel and into the elevator designated for the penthouse. No one spoke during the ascent and the tension in the cubicle swelled until Anna felt as if it had consumed most of the oxygen. She caught Kat surreptitiously wiping away a tear and touched Kat's arm. "Are you okay?"

Kat took a ragged breath. "No."

Pierce stiffened. The elevator doors opened directly into the living room of the suite. He exited. Anna and Kat followed.

He headed straight to the bar—a full bar, no minibar here. "Drink?"

Both Anna and Kat declined.

"I have something to say and I want you to listen," Kat said in a rush that sounded nothing like her professional news correspondent voice. "First, I know you don't believe me, but I really wasn't trying to trap you into marriage or extort money from you when I got pregnant. All the money you've sent has gone into an account for Graham. He'll get it when he turns twenty-one."

"If not for marriage or money then why?" Pierce said through clenched teeth.

"Two and a half years ago I had a close call. I never…I never told you how close I came to not coming home. And then a few months later Peter was killed, and I had to face the mortality rate in our business. I realized there was a good chance I would die as my brother had doing this kind of job. And then what? What would I leave behind other than a few old news reels?

"I got this crazy idea that I needed a child to prove that I had been here, that I'd lived on this planet, that I had made a difference. And I decided to get pregnant. Not the smartest decision now that I look back on it with hindsight, but at the time…it seemed like the only one."

Anna searched Pierce's face for his reaction. Only the telltale signs of pinched nostrils and bunched jaw muscles revealed his tension.

Kat wrapped her arms around her middle. "You and I…we were both losing interest in our on-again-off-again relationship. I figured it was only a matter of time before we ended it. And you were the best candidate to father my child. So I went off the pill and as soon as I confirmed I was pregnant I stopped calling you when I came to town. I was never going to tell you about the baby. And I never expected you to marry me or support us. If my colleague hadn't blown it with that on-air announcement you would never have known. I know you don't believe me. But those are the facts."

Anna could see the truth written all over Kat's pale, strained face and in the slight tremor of her hands. She handed the woman a tissue. "I believe you."

Kat gave her a wobbly smile. "Thank you. This time I had nineteen days of captivity to think about my career, my life and my death. I didn't know if I'd make it out alive or if the radicals who held me would make an example of me. I wondered what would happen to Graham if I never came home. When I planned this I guess I just didn't think it through. The sleepless nights. The child care issues. My ineptness.

"I'm a damned good correspondent—one of the best in my field. But parenting... I am far from being the best mom. I make so many mistakes with him. The worst mistake is denying Graham the security of knowing whether or not Mommy will come home."

"Change jobs," Pierce stated firmly. "Take an anchor position."

Kat shook her head. "I can't rest until I know who killed my brother. That means I can't promise I won't go back over there. And because of that I want you—"

She hiccupped, bowed her head and covered her face with her hands, then gathered herself and lifted her head. Tears streamed down her cheeks. "You offered joint custody. But I—I think G-Graham would be better off with you."

Stunned, Anna watched Kat struggle with her emotions. Anna couldn't imagine ever voluntarily walking away from Cody. She moved forward and placed a reassuring arm around Kat's shoulders. "We all make mistakes, Kat. That's part of learning to be a parent."

Fresh tears rolled down Kat's cheeks. "I'm glad Graham is going to have you, but I think it's best for him not to have me blowing in and out of his life and confusing him. The day care failure this time…I searched so long to find just the right person and I thought she was reliable. What if something like that happens again? I'm not a good mother. That's why I want—" She gulped once, twice, a third time. "Pierce, I want you to take full custody of Graham. Please."

"Of course. If that's what you want I will assume full custody," he answered without hesitation. "But Anna is right. We all make mistakes. She also taught me that we all need to be connected to someone. I lost that connection with my parents, Sean and Hank. And I stupidly thought that by not letting myself care about anyone else my life would be better, because if I didn't love anyone I couldn't be hurt by losing them. But I was wrong.

"Any time or love you can give our son will be better than denying him your presence altogether. A child can never have too many people who love him.

"We'll do whatever you want legally, Kat, but know my door will always be open. You can visit Graham any time you want and for as long as you want. I would hate to see him lose his mother's and grandfather's love."

Anna's heart swelled so much it nearly choked her. Happy tears pooled in her eyes. She pressed a hand to her chest and blinked.

Pierce got it. He actually understood what it meant to open his heart. He was learning—albeit in baby steps—to be as generous with his heart as he was with his money.

And if he could love his son, that meant he might have room for her and Cody.

Kat nodded. "Thank you. Thank you so much."

And then she turned and fled.

Pierce turned to Anna. She smiled. "That was exactly the

right thing to do. You have just embarked on a wonderful journey, and there's nowhere I'd rather be than by your side as you learn how fulfilling the reward of giving love can be." She stepped closer to him.

"I love you, Pierce. And yes, I'll marry you and build a family with you."

He pulled her into his arms and brushed his lips across hers. "I'll make damned sure you don't regret it. I love you, Anna Aronson. I promise to be the best possible husband and father I can be."

Epilogue

A nna tugged one more tendril free from her upswept hair and turned her head to study the effect. It would do.

She loved nights like this when she could don a designer gown and spend an evening with her husband—especially when it was for a good cause like the Hollister scholarship banquet.

But then Pierce had filled the past two years with Cinderella moments like this. He'd begun by giving her a fairy-tale wedding that even her mother had approved of, then he'd swept her and their boys off to tour the best European museums, allowing Anna to gorge herself on fine art. After their honeymoon he'd brought them to his exquisite Arizona home which he'd had totally childproofed during their absence.

The silence caught her attention. "Pierce?" No reply.

She left the luxurious bathroom, but Pierce wasn't in their bedroom. Nor was he in his walk-in closet. She checked the gold and diamond watch he'd given her after she'd delivered their daughter. Her heart still hitched each time she recalled his words. "This watch signifies how precious our time together has become to me."

She blinked back the happy tears and focused on the dial. The limo would be here any minute. Where was her missing husband? If she had to hazard a guess...

She headed down the hall to the nursery and stopped at the door. A smile tugged her lips. She should have known she'd find him standing over the crib. Again.

"Pierce, we're going to be late."

"I'm not sure I'm ready to leave her," he said without looking away from their daughter. "This will be our first night out since we brought her home. I hadn't expected it to be so difficult."

Her worries about his workaholic tendencies had been unfounded. He raced home each night and never missed having dinner with his family and he never ever took work with him on vacation the way her father had.

Pierce's brow pleated. "Are you sure Kat's up for this?"

Anna joined him by the crib. "Kat's come a long way, and you know how much she loves spending time with the children. She can handle two healthy boys and one perfect month-old angel for a few hours."

"Shawna is perfect." He moved the stuffed pink bunny to the opposite end of the crib and stroked their daughter's rosy-cheeked face.

"Yes, she is. And stop trying to wake her so that you can say good-night again." Anna loved that he'd become such a protective—almost overprotective—papa of their boys and the baby they'd named after his brother. When Pierce had opened his heart, he'd opened it Grand Canyon wide.

Pierce glanced at her, then did a double-take. His hazel eyes widened and raked her from head to toe. His chest swelled as his breath hissed slowly inward through clenched teeth. The hunger tightening his features made her flush hot all over. Desire curled like smoke in her belly. Though she slept in his arms every night it seemed like forever since she'd taken him into her body, and she needed him. Badly.

She took his shoulders and turned him slightly so she could tie his black bowtie. He looked so delicious in his crisp white shirt and tuxedo pants that she almost wanted to forget their engagement and drag him to bed.

Once the tie was straight she smoothed her hands across his chest, bumping over his tiny, tight nipples. Hers puckered in response. Then she forced herself to step back before she gave in to the urge to smear her red lipstick across his mouth and stroked a hand across the waist of her sapphire blue evening gown.

"It feels good to wear something besides maternity clothes or sensible teacher garb."

He traced one of the curls streaming from her nape over her shoulder and the gentle rasp of his fingertip made her shiver. "You're the one who insisted on going back to work while the boys were in preschool."

So she had. "And I love it. I have the best of both worlds—a fulfilling part-time job and my mommy time. I adore my students, and I have missed them while I've been on maternity leave this semester. I'm looking forward to returning in January. Have I thanked you often enough for helping me land that position?"

A wicked grin curved his mouth. "Depends on how you plan to show your gratitude. You look very, very sexy tonight, Mrs. Hollister."

When he spoke in that lower octave and looked at her as if he'd like to gobble her up she felt very desirable indeed. She cupped his freshly shaven cheek, relishing the smoothness of his skin almost as much as she missed the rasp of his evening beard against her most sensitive parts.

"Perhaps after the banquet you can show me how sexy."

His dark eyebrows hiked slightly and hope glimmered in his eyes. "It's not too soon?"

"The doctor gave me the all-clear at my appointment today."

His nostrils flared. He wound his arms around her waist and lowered his head. His hot body pressed hers and his lips were a breath away from her mouth when the thunder of little feet raced into the room. Pierce gave her a frustrated smile and released her.

"Pick me up, Momma," soon-to-be three-year-old Graham demanded.

Anna took one look at his food-smeared face and hesitated.

"Come to Daddy, sport. We don't want to mess up Mommy's pretty dress." Pierce scooped up his son, who immediately buried his grubby face against his father's shoulder.

Anna winced. "Your shirt—"

"My jacket will cover it. You on the other hand…." His gaze roved over her expanded cleavage. Her pregnancy followed by nursing their daughter had expanded her breasts. "That dress is too spectacular to have to change it. It stays on until I take it off."

Her pulse skipped in anticipation.

Cody came tromping into the room. Pierce picked him up, juggling both boys as if he'd been doing it for years. "Let's get you boys cleaned up."

Kat swept into the room looking elegant even in her sweats and baggy T-shirt. Anna had to admit she'd been leery about becoming friends with one of Pierce's past lovers, but not once in the past two years during Kat's almost bi-monthly visits had she witnessed a single untoward incident between her husband and his ex.

"The limo just pulled up. I've got the dynamic duo. You two need to go. Have a great time. Stay as late as you like. And yes, Pierce, I will keep my cell phone handy if you need to make a video call to check on your children."

His cheeks darkened. "I've only done that once."

"Twice," Kat and Anna said in unison and grinned at each other.

But Anna loved him for it.

He handed over the boys and held out his hand. Anna placed hers in his, letting the heat of his palm warm her soul. She would never have believed it two years ago, but there was nowhere she'd rather be and no one she'd rather be with than the man who'd once had an armor-plated personality.

* * * * *

PASSION

Harlequin® *Desire*

COMING NEXT MONTH
AVAILABLE JUNE 12, 2012

#2161 HIS MARRIAGE TO REMEMBER
The Good, the Bad and the Texan
Kathie DeNosky

#2162 A VERY PRIVATE MERGER
Dynasties: The Kincaids
Day Leclaire

#2163 THE PATERNITY PROMISE
Billionaires and Babies
Merline Lovelace

#2164 IMPOSSIBLE TO RESIST
The Men of Wolff Mountain
Janice Maynard

#2165 THE SHEIKH'S REDEMPTION
Desert Knights
Olivia Gates

#2166 A TANGLED AFFAIR
The Pearl House
Fiona Brand

REQUEST YOUR FREE BOOKS!

2 FREE NOVELS PLUS 2 FREE GIFTS!

Harlequin

Desire

ALWAYS POWERFUL, PASSIONATE AND PROVOCATIVE

YES! Please send me 2 FREE Harlequin Desire® novels and my 2 FREE gifts (gifts are worth about $10). After receiving them, if I don't wish to receive any more books, I can return the shipping statement marked "cancel." If I don't cancel, I will receive 6 brand-new novels every month and be billed just $4.30 per book in the U.S. or $4.99 per book in Canada. That's a saving of at least 14% off the cover price! It's quite a bargain! Shipping and handling is just 50¢ per book in the U.S. and 75¢ per book in Canada.* I understand that accepting the 2 free books and gifts places me under no obligation to buy anything. I can always return a shipment and cancel at any time. Even if I never buy another book, the two free books and gifts are mine to keep forever.

225/326 HDN FEF3

Name	(PLEASE PRINT)

Address	Apt. #

City	State/Prov.	Zip/Postal Code

Signature (if under 18, a parent or guardian must sign)

Mail to the **Reader Service:**
IN U.S.A.: P.O. Box 1867, Buffalo, NY 14240-1867
IN CANADA: P.O. Box 609, Fort Erie, Ontario L2A 5X3

Not valid for current subscribers to Harlequin Desire books.

Want to try two free books from another line?
Call 1-800-873-8635 or visit www.ReaderService.com.

* Terms and prices subject to change without notice. Prices do not include applicable taxes. Sales tax applicable in N.Y. Canadian residents will be charged applicable taxes. Offer not valid in Quebec. This offer is limited to one order per household. All orders subject to credit approval. Credit or debit balances in a customer's account(s) may be offset by any other outstanding balance owed by or to the customer. Please allow 4 to 6 weeks for delivery. Offer available while quantities last.

Your Privacy—The Reader Service is committed to protecting your privacy. Our Privacy Policy is available online at www.ReaderService.com or upon request from the Reader Service.

We make a portion of our mailing list available to reputable third parties that offer products we believe may interest you. If you prefer that we not exchange your name with third parties, or if you wish to clarify or modify your communication preferences, please visit us at www.ReaderService.com/consumerchoice or write to us at Reader Service Preference Service, P.O. Box 9062, Buffalo, NY 14269. Include your complete name and address.

HDES11B

red-hot reads

Fall under the spell of fan-favorite author

Leslie Kelly

Workaholic Mimi Burdette thinks she's satisfied dating the handsome man her father has picked out for her. But when sexy firefighter Xander McKinley moves into her apartment building, Mimi finds herself becoming…distracted. When Mimi opens a fortune cookie predicting who will be the man of her dreams, then starts having erotic dreams, she never imagines Xander is having the same dreams! Until they come together and bring those dreams to life.

Blazing Midsummer Nights

The magic begins June 2012

Saddle up with Harlequin® series books this summer and find a cowboy for every mood!

Available wherever books are sold.

www.Harlequin.com

HB79693

USA TODAY *bestselling author Kathie DeNosky presents the first book in her brand-new miniseries,* THE GOOD, THE BAD AND THE TEXAN.

HIS MARRIAGE TO REMEMBER

Available June 2012 from Harlequin® Desire!

Brianna wasn't sure Sam would want her here. After all, they were just one signature away from a divorce. But until the dissolution of their marriage was final, they were still legally married, which meant she was needed here.

As she turned to go through the hospital's Intensive Care Unit doors to Sam's room, Brianna bit her lower lip to keep it from trembling. Even though she and Sam were ending their relationship, the very last thing she wanted was to see him harmed.

"Does your head hurt, Sam?" she asked.

He reached for her hand. "Don't worry, sweetheart. I'm going to be just fine. If you'll get my clothes, I'll get dressed and we can go home. Hell, I'll even let you play nurse."

Why was Sam insisting they go home together? She had moved out of the ranch house three months ago. His obvious lack of memory bothered her. She needed to speak to the doctor about it right away. "Try to get some rest. We'll deal with everything in the morning."

Sam didn't look happy, but he finally nodded. Then he pinned her with his piercing blue gaze. "Are you doing all right?"

Confused, she nodded. "I'm doing okay. Why do you ask?"

"You told me you were going to get one of those pregnancy tests at the drug store," Sam said, giving her hand a gentle squeeze. "Were we successful? Are you pregnant?"

A cold, sinking feeling settled in the pit of her stomach. He didn't remember. She had miscarried in her seventh week, and that had been almost six months ago. Something was definitely wrong.

"No, I'm not pregnant," she said. "Now, get some rest. I'll be in later to check on you."

"It's going to be hard to do without you beside me," he said, giving her a grin.

Some things never changed, she thought as she left to find the neurologist. The sun rose in the east. The ocean rushed to shore. And Sam Rafferty could make her knees weak with nothing more than his sexy-as-sin smile.

What will Brianna do if Sam never remembers the truth?

Find out in Kathie DeNosky's new novel
HIS MARRIAGE TO REMEMBER

Available June 2012 from Harlequin® Desire!

Harlequin *Presents*®

Live like royalty…if only for a day.

Discover a passionate duet from

Jane Porter

When blue blood runs hot…

When Hannah Smith agrees to switch places for a day with Princess Emmeline, a woman who looks exactly like her, she soon ends up in some royal hot water. Especially when Emmeline disappears and Hannah finds herself with a country to run and a gorgeous, off-limits king she's quickly falling for—Emmeline's fiancé! What's a fake princess to do?

NOT FIT FOR A KING?
Available June 2012

And coming soon in July
HIS MAJESTY'S MISTAKE

Available wherever books are sold.

SPECIAL EDITION

Life, Love and Family

USA TODAY bestselling author

Marie Ferrarella

enchants readers in

ONCE UPON A MATCHMAKER

Micah Muldare's aunt is worried that her nephew is going to wind up alone in his old age...but this matchmaking mama has just the thing! When Micah finds himself accused of theft, defense lawyer Tracy Ryan agrees to help him as a favor to his aunt, but soon finds herself drawn to more than just his case. Will Micah open up his heart and realize Tracy is his match?

Available June 2012

Saddle up with Harlequin® series books this summer and find a cowboy for every mood!

Available wherever books are sold.

www.Harlequin.com

HSE65674